Praise for
Shivers, Scares, and Chills and Vonnie Winslow Crist

"Usually, follow ups to successful books suffer from a sophomore slump. With her new collection, *Shivers, Scares, and Chills*, Vonnie Winslow Crist has not only equaled the spine-tingling delights and frights of the first book in this series, she has surpassed them. From the hair-raising opening tale ("Rabbits") to the concluding piece ("Field Trip"), Crist had me wide-eyed. These very short stories are geared to preteenagers and teenagers, but holy cow, they had this old guy glued to his seat. Her ability to stimulate the readers imagination and to invoke ghastly visuals is superb. And man, those endings... So, thank you Vonnie Winslow Crist, my grandkids will be so happy to know that I've got a brand new book of stories that will have them leaving the lights on at bedtime."

~ Tony Tremblay,
Author of *The Moore House* and *The Damage Done*

"Vonnie Winslow Crist's SS&C contains nothing but fear, fun, and, oh yeah, some awesome illustrations! These are the type of bedtime stories that I craved decades ago and rarely found. Today's young readers have reason to celebrate. Bravo Vonnie!"

~ Douglas Draa,
Editor of *Weirdbook Magazine*

"You're on that one carnival ride that you always dread. It dips and spins you, whirls you around, and then you turn upside down. Yet somehow it feels good! It's the feeling you get when reading a well-written scary tale. If you like that feeling, you will *love* Vonnie Winslow Crist's *Shivers, Scares, and Chills*. From flittermice in the chimney, to black dogs and kelpies, underwater creatures with tentacles that grab, and gargoyles that serve an oh-so-good purpose, this book will not disappoint. The pit of your stomach will surely jiggle, your heart will race, and there's a chance you may not be able to swallow down that lump in your throat. Join me. Tap into your deepest emotions and vulnerabilities. I promise, you won't be disappointed."

~ Lois Szymanski,
Author of dozens of books for young readers,
including *The Gettysburg Ghost Gang*,
co-written by Shelley Sykes.

"Crist's second volume of bedtime stories is every bit as delightfully wicked a collection as her *Shivers, Scares, and Goosebumps*. Like the first, it's beautifully illustrated, each image must have taken months to complete. I love that the author doesn't 'write down' to what we might say is a child's reading level. She wisely relies on the story to carry along interest for meaning of words such as 'cuspid,' 'gnarled,' or 'entombed.' A fascinating story is a great way to enhance a child's vocabulary. But what I love most are the twisty endings, some with a moral and some are just plain bad luck. For instance, the kid who was at the wrong place at the wrong time gets eaten by a goblin. We know that such tales are best read aloud, the scarier the better! A must buy and keep for your child's library!"

~ Marge Simon,
Bram Stoker Award winning author and poet

"Vonnie Winslow Crist is a chameleon of a writer—as a reader, you never know where her tales will take you—yet there's always one thing you can count on: top-notch storytelling."

~ Richard Chizmar,
New York Times bestselling author of the Gwendy's Button
Box Trilogy and *The Girl on the Porch*

“As a writer, editor, and artist, Vonnie is a gem of our science fiction-fantasy community.”

~ Tom M. Doyle,
award-winning author of the American Craft series,
Border Crosser, and *The Wizard of Macatawa*

Shivers, Scares, and Chills

Written and Illustrated by
Vonnie Winslow Crist

From
Dark Owl Publishing, LLC

Arizona

ISBN 978-1-951716-42-4

Cover and interior illustrations by Vonnie Winslow Crist.
Cover design by Dark Owl Publishing.

Visit us on our website at:
www.darkowlpublishing.com

Books by Vonnie Winslow Crist

The Chronicles of Lifthrasir
The Enchanted Dagger
Beyond the Sheercliffs

Novelette
Murder on Marawa Prime

Story Collections
Dragon Rain
Beneath Raven's Wing
Owl Light
The Greener Forest

Young Adult and Middle Grade
Shivers, Scares, and Goosebumps
Shivers, Scares, and Chills

Children's
Leprechaun Cake & Other Tales

Poetry Collections
River of Stars
Essential Fables

More Young Readers Books from Dark Owl Publishing

Shivers, Scares, and Goosebumps
The first collection of spooky stories
designed to be read under the covers!
both written and illustrated by Vonnie Winslow Crist

Annette: A Big, Hairy Mom
A touching story of a boy and
his motherly friend, a Sasquatch.
both written and illustrated by John S. McFarland

Annette: A Big, Hairy Grandma
The romping next adventure about
everyone's favorite Sasquatch!
both written and illustrated by John S. McFarland

In addition, all books from Dark Owl Publishing are appropriate for at least teenagers to read.

Please see the Young Readers Bookstore page on our website for details on age appropriateness.

www.darkowlpublishing.com/the-yr-bookstore

For Ernie,
Tim and Dawn,
Phil, Kristin, Nathaniel and Gabriel,
Melissa and Aria,
And all those who enjoy
Shivery, scary, goosebump-filled tales.

Table of Contents

©2024 Vonnie Winslow Crist

Rabbits

"The teeth!—the teeth!—they were here, and there, and everywhere..."
– Berenice

On a warm April afternoon, wearing their safety glasses, Kelly, her brother, Barry, and their parents observed the solar eclipse. Another solar eclipse wouldn't be visible in the central part of the United States for twenty years. So they felt lucky to have seen it.

The day after the solar eclipse, Kelly noticed wildlife near her family's house acting strangely. A loft of pigeons lined up, side by side, on their house's rain gutter and cooed in unison. But their usually placid calls sounded hollow and ghostly.

Rather than gather breadcrumbs alone, sparrows arrived in a host of about fifteen birds. The sparrows didn't study Kelly with bright, shiny eyes while they ate the crusts she'd tossed onto the grass. Instead, their eyes were covered with a filmy glaze. She was amazed the birds saw well enough to find the bread.

The next day, the lone spider who'd woven a web in a rosebush near their home's backdoor was joined by a cluster of its kin. Kelly's skin prickled at the sight of the fibers in the center of the web crawling with hundreds of spiders. As she studied the web, the arachnids raised their front feet as if challenging her to touch them.

The lone mouse that occasionally scurried down their

driveway to the trashcan was joined by the rest of its nest. The throng of small rodents looked back at Kelly. They snapped their jaws and flicked their tails.

Even the ants seemed changed. Rather than march across the sidewalk in single file, they swarmed in a small army across the concrete slabs. Kelly had the distinct feeling if she stepped in their path, the ants would cover and then consume her.

Spooked by the animals' behavior, Kelly ran inside the house.

"I think something weird is going on with the birds and bugs," she told her brother.

"It's just your imagination," said Barry. He barely lifted his eyes from the book he was reading. "Go back outside and face your irrational fears."

"I'm not afraid," Kelly replied as she turned toward the door. "I just think something is wrong with the animals."

Barry grunted at her.

"You're being silly," Kelly told herself as she walked down the porch steps. "It is just your imagination."

She heard rustling under the back porch, bent down, and looked beneath the wooden floorboards. A dead rabbit was stretched out on the dirt. Before she could call out for her brother, the rabbit rolled over and stood on its partially decomposed legs.

Kelly gasped and stepped back. Reaching to her left, she grabbed a garden rake from where it leaned against the house.

Could the bunny's reanimation have been caused by the solar eclipse? she wondered.

Holding the rake with both hands, she warned, "Stay back."

But the half-decayed rabbit ignored her words and kept creeping toward her. Then, the raggedy creature gnashed its teeth and snarled.

Surprised at how much larger bunny teeth appeared without skin around the mouth, she thought, *Those incisors could do real damage.*

Rapid clicking from behind her caused Kelly to whirl around. She spotted more than a dozen zombified bunnies with empty eye sockets surrounding her.

When she shouted for Barry, the fluffle of dead rabbits jumped on her.

A few seconds later, her brother hurried out the door. Before him he saw rotting rabbits biting, tearing, and chewing on Kelly.

"Get off her," he yelled.

Too late, Barry realized he was next, when the bunnies turned toward him, smiling hungrily with their nasty, sharp, zombie teeth.

©2024

Flittermice

"It is nothing but the wind in the chimney…"
– The Tell-Tale Heart

"Let's go up to my bedroom," Lee-Lee told Cammie.

"Okay!" agreed Cammie as they clamored up the stairs to the third floor.

"It's this one," said Lee-Lee. She pushed open the door on the left and led her into a large room with a fireplace on the far wall.

"Wow! You've got your own fireplace." Cammie crossed the room, knelt down, and looked inside the firebox. "Does it work?"

"No." Lee-Lee flopped on the twin bed nearest to the door. "Dad says it needs to be cleaned by a chimney sweep and maybe repaired."

"Too bad." Cammie stood. "It would be cool to tell ghost stories tonight in front of the fireplace."

"Who needs a fire?" Lee-Lee grinned. "I'll tell you one right now."

"Sure." Cammie sat on the bed nearest the fireplace facing her friend. "But is it a true story?"

"It's a true as they come," Lee-Lee assured her. Then, her friend began the tale.

"This room used to belong to my Great Aunt Pauline. She never married, and lived with my grandparents until she died two years ago. Even when she was really old, Aunt Pauline had long hair. Every night, she'd sit on that bench in front of the vanity." Lee-Lee pointed at a vanity with curved legs opposite the beds before continuing. "She'd brush her long hair one hundred times before going to sleep."

"What's so scary about that?" asked Cammie.

"Nothing," replied her friend. "Now, comes the scary part." Lowering her voice to a whisper, Lee-Lee finished the tale. "Beginning the night after Aunt Pauline died, I started hearing brushing sounds at sundown. I knew it was Aunt Pauline's ghost brushing her hair. And sometimes in the middle of the night, I still hear her ghost."

Cammie laughed. "So, am I going to see her ghost tonight?"

"Maybe," said Lee-Lee. "But if you ask my parents about the brushing noise, they'll tell you it's nothing but the wind or flittermice."

"Flittermice?" Cammie wasn't sure she wanted to know what a flittermouse was.

"It's what my grandmom calls bats," explained Lee-Lee. "But don't worry. Dad closed the fireplace's damper. So, even if there are flittermice in the chimney, they can't get into my bedroom.

"Great," said Cammie in what she hoped sounded like a carefree voice. If she was honest, Cammie was afraid of bats. Maybe this sleepover wasn't such a good idea. But not wanting to be a fraidy-cat, she said nothing.

***

At sundown, Cammie heard the rustling sound her friend had spoken of. A few minutes later, it stopped.

"See," said Lee-Lee, "nothing but flittermice."

Somewhat relieved, Cammie continued to watch movies and eat popcorn with Lee-Lee. A little after midnight, Lee-Lee's mom told them to turn off the lights and go to sleep.

As they rested in their beds with moonlight streaming through the windows, her friend said, "Good night. Sleep tight. Don't let Aunt Pauline scare you tonight."

They both laughed, snuggled beneath their covers, and drifted into dreamland.

***

Hours later, a brushing noise awakened Cammie. She sat up and stared at the vanity bench. There, brushing her long, pale hair, was a woman in an ankle-length nightgown.

"Aunt Pauline?" she asked in a small voice.

The woman in white stood, glided to Cammie's bed, and whispered, "Yes, dear. Would you like me to also brush your hair?"

"No," said Cammie. "No, no, no." Each time she said the word, "No," her voice grew louder until she woke up Lee-Lee.

"What's wrong?" asked her friend between yawns.

"Aunt Pauline is here," said Cammie.

"It's just a ghost story," said Lee-Lee. "Go back to sleep."

Cammie pointed to the old-fashioned hairbrush resting on her bedspread.

"No, it's *not* just a story. It's *not* just flittermice. Aunt Pauline *is* here," she told her friend. "In fact, she's standing behind you *right now*!"*

*If you are reading this story out loud, you can point to someone who is listening when you say the last line.

© 2024

Redcap

"This ghoul-haunted woodland..."
– Ulalume – A Ballad

"It's not personal," explained a thickset, mannish creature as he dragged Lonnie deeper into the woods. "But my cap has faded."

"I don't understand," cried Lonnie. "Who are you? What do you want?"

He struggled to remain upright. Told by his uncle to stay in the back yard, Lonnie had nevertheless wandered into the woods. He'd been less than fifteen feet into the forest when he'd been grabbed.

"I'm Goblin Redcap," answered the creature. "I needs some dye."

Lonnie fought to loosen the grip of the goblin's clawed hand as he was pulled deeper into the wildwood. But Redcap's hold was unbreakable.

"Please," Lonnie managed to say.

"I am pleased," responded Redcap.

The goblin's iron boots clanked as Lonnie and he descended a staircase into the cellar of an abandoned house hidden behind a thicket of sticker bushes and dogwoods. "You appears to be a healthy lad. There should be plenty of blood for the dyeing."

"Blood!" exclaimed Lonnie. *Think*, he said to himself.

"The goblin whistled a lively tune as he kicked some branches away from an old tub.

"Listen, if you let me go, I can buy you some red dye at the grocery store," offered Lonnie, still trying to loosen Redcap's grip on his arm. "Then I'll bring it back to you. One box should be enough to dye your cap four or five times. Maybe more."

"Nope," replied the goblin. "A red bird in the hand is worth more than four or five red birds in the bush." He chuckled at his clever twist of the old saying.

Redcap held Lonnie above the rust-stained tub with his left hand. With his right hand, he lifted his pikestaff.

"Any last words?" asked the goblin.

"Wait!" yelled Lonnie.

"Nope," said Redcap as he swung his weapon.

Later, the goblin propped Lonnie's bloodless body against the trunk of an oak aside a stream. Then Redcap admired his reflection in the gurgling water. Delighted with the brilliant scarlet color of his cap, he smiled.

"Boy's bad luck was my good luck," he told dozens of skeletons propped against the trunks of nearby trees.

When the skeletons didn't respond, Redcap tapped his cap with his thick fingers, turned, and strode away.

"See you again soon," called the goblin over his shoulder.

Redcap knew blood faded quickly. He'd be back within six months' time after another dyeing.

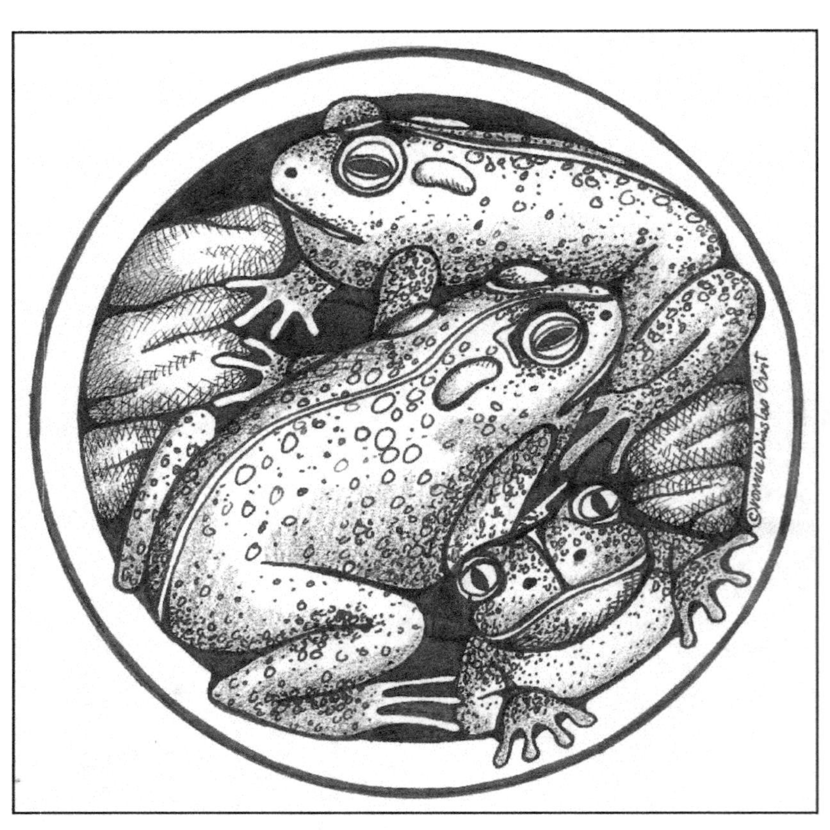
©Vonnie Winslow Crist

Toads

"Where the toad and the newt encamp..."
– Dream-Land

"Watch out for that circle of toadstools," Tabitha warned her friend Kathleen as they walked below the arching branches of sugar maples and dogwoods.

"You mean these mushrooms?" said Kathleen. She kicked several of the toadstools. After the fungi broke into pieces, Kathleen stomped on the bigger chunks. "There won't be any toads sitting on these mushrooms now," she sneered.

"It's not just the toads you have to worry about." Tabitha surveyed the damage. "That was a fairy ring. There are other creatures who might be offended."

"Like elves and dwarves?" Kathleen laughed. Raising her left hand, she made a beckoning motion toward the thicker part of the forest. "Anyone in there willing to stop me from smashing the rest of this mushroom circle?"

"I am," croaked a deep voice.

Tabitha and Kathleen froze.

From between two trees stepped a toad-headed goblin.

"Rather than destroy it, I think you might need that toadstool to sit upon," growled the goblin as it tapped Kathleen on the shoulder with a webbed hand.

Faster than a toad's tongue can flick out and grab a beetle, Kathleen morphed into a small hop toad.

"You'd better leave," the toad-head goblin warned Tabitha. "Unless you want to be an amphibian, too."

"No!" gasped Tabitha. She spun around and, careful to avoid any mushrooms, dashed out of the woods.

That night when she stepped outside to look at the stars, Tabitha spotted a small hop toad beside her porch.

"Kathleen?" she said. "Is that you?"

The little toad chirped, hopped closer, and nodded.

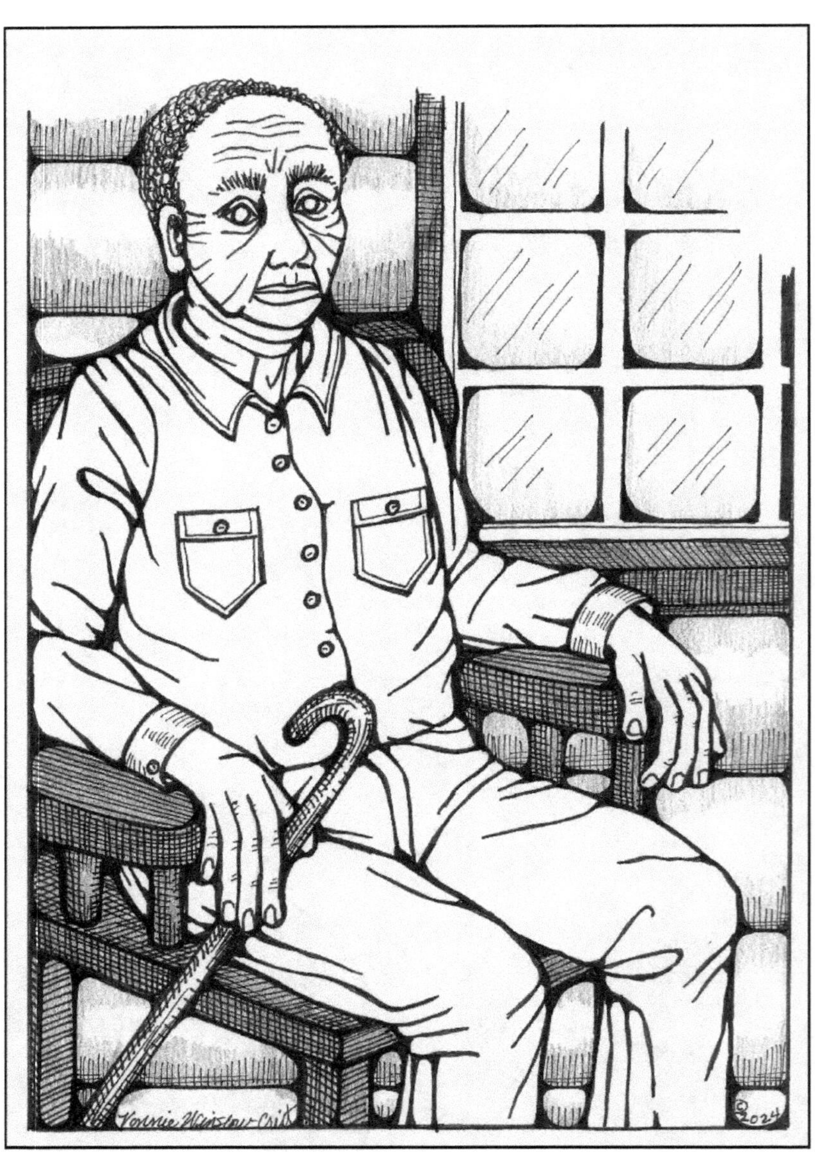
Vonnie Winslow-Crist
© 2024

Marbles

"...I do not expect you to believe..."
– The Murders in the Rue Morgue

William drew a circle with chalk on the sidewalk at the bottom of his home's front porch steps. After dumping out his marbles, he selected his favorite green glass shooter. Since he only had a few minutes to shoot marbles before dinner, William didn't go across the street to see if his friend, Kathleen, could play.

A glance up at the porch confirmed he was alone. His grandfather's rocking chair was empty. William rubbed his eyes with the back of his sleeve. The chair and the cane resting on its seat were the only reminders of Pappy left on the porch.

Distracted by thoughts of his grandfather and yesterday's funeral, William didn't notice the three older boys behind him until one of them spoke.

"Nice looking marbles, Willy Boy," said Talbot Simpson.

"Thanks," replied William as he inched away from Talbot and his friends. He slid his green shooter into his pocket.

"I think you should put those marbles in their bag and give them to me." Talbot took a step closer and continued, "Then, I won't have to beat you up to get them."

The two boys behind Talbot snickered.

"And don't forget to put the shooter you slipped into your pocket in the bag, too." Talbot crossed his arms in front of his chest. At the same time, he kicked William. "Hurry up,

Willy Boy. I don't like to be kept waiting."

Outnumbered three to one by bigger kids, William knew he didn't have much choice. If Pappy had been there, Talbot and his buddies would never have bothered him. But his grandfather was dead and buried. Resigned to give the neighborhood bully his marbles, William started to gather the shiny globes and drop them into their bag.

"Faster!" ordered Talbot as he kicked William again.

Suddenly, William heard several loud thwacks and saw Talbot fall to the ground. Looking up, he saw Talbot's friends trying to block Pappy's cane. The cane swung around all by itself, whistled through the air, and struck the bullies again and again.

Talbot crawled to his feet as his friends took off. He glared at William and balled up his fists.

Before Talbot could hit William, an old man's voice warned, "Talbot Simpson, I'll be watching you and your friends. Don't force me to come back again because of your bullying. For next time, I might forget to stop after a few thwacks with my cane."

Then, Pappy winked into view. He was dressed in his burial suit and shiny shoes. In his wrinkled hands he twirled his cane.

Talbot's mouth dropped open. He yelled, spun around, then ran down the street as if every ghost in the graveyard was chasing him.

"That should do it," said Pappy before smiling at William and vanishing, the cane dropping to the ground.

Wishing he could have had more time with his grandfather, William gathered up his marbles, picked up Pappy's cane, and brushed the graveyard soil from the sidewalk. Then he climbed onto the porch.

While placing the cane on his grandfather's chair, William murmured, "Thank you."

"You are welcome," whispered the wind as it caused the chair to rock.

©2024

Feeding the Fish

"The quiet waters had closed placidly over their victim…"
– The Assignation

Standing on the observation deck, Annabel tossed bread to catfish churning the water behind the reservoir's upper dam. She was mesmerized by their glazed eyes, thrashing tails, and hungry mouths.

In the chilly, green water, the whiskered fish looked like shadows curling around one another. But Annabel spotted something paler swimming among the catfish. To get a better look, she crawled under the safety chains. Then, she hurried down the concrete steps until she was at the water's edge.

"Get back up here," shouted her older brother, Eddie. "Dad said to stay away from the edge of the water."

"I'm fine." Annabel looked up at Eddie.

He was scowling. Muttering something under his breath, he slipped under the safety chains.

"Seriously, Annabel. Dad's going to be mad," said her brother. "He told us there were all sorts of dangers near the dam, and to stay on the observation deck."

She waved her hand at Eddie but ignored his words. Instead, she knelt and studied the dozens of catfish gazing up at her.

Without warning, a whitish tentacle flew from the water. As the tentacle encircled her ankle, Annabel called her brother's name. Before Eddie could run down the steps and grab her arms, she was yanked into the chilly water.

As the tentacled monster drew her further below the surface, Annabel gazed up at her brother's face. She tried to yell, "Look out!" But Annabel only managed to swallow a mouthful of water. For a second beast, which was the twin of the monster pulling her into its toothy mouth, was reaching its limbs toward Eddie.

Suddenly, a sucker-covered tentacle exploded from the water and grabbed her brother.*

But Annabel didn't hear Eddie yell for help. She was already in the reservoir monster's belly.

*If you are reading this story to someone else, you can grab their arm when you say this.

©2024
Vonnie Winslow Crist

Dowsing

"...I vowed revenge."
– The Cask of Amontillado

"How much are you charging me, water witch, for finding where to drill the well?" asked Roderick Legrand.

New owner of the corner property on the road where Drucilla Darkwander lived, Roderick was known for being a shrewd businessman. Rather than hire an expensive scientific know-it-all, he'd asked Drucilla to use her dowsing skills to find where to drill for water. When the well-driller Roderick had hired struck water on the first try, he laughed and rubbed the palms of his hands together.

"Lucky guess, Drucilla!" he said. Then, after putting on his jacket, he added, "Drilling only once saves me time and money."

The well-driller and his two helpers glanced from Roderick to Drucilla. They shook their heads. The helpers, Fraser and Jonesy Testerman, lived next door to Drucilla. Last winter, they had learned the hard way not to offend her.

"Pay whatever you think my dowsing skills are worth, Roderick," Drucilla Darkwander told the real estate developer. She slipped her dowsing rods into her shoulder bag. Then she picked up her black cat, Shadow.

Though she never officially charged for water witching, rune casting, or herb craft, Drucilla expected fair compensation. Accurate well drilling saved thousands of dollars. Good runic advice was priceless. And, she believed, some natural cures were healthier than store bought medicines. Of course, others disagreed.

"Didn't take you, that scrawny cat, and your bent wires long to pick this spot." Roderick leafed through the money in his wallet. "So I don't suppose I owe you much."

Drucilla said nothing. She held Shadow and studied the owner of Legrand Land Development.

Roderick pursed his lips. He pulled out fifty dollars, shook his head, then pushed a ten-dollar and twenty-dollar bill back into his leather billfold. After rubbing his chin, Roderick handed the dowser a twenty-dollar bill.

Ungrateful penny pincher, thought Drucilla. But she said, "Thank you, Mr. Legrand. You know where to find me if you need anything else."

With a wave of his hand, Roderick dismissed the water witch.

Drucilla noticed the well-driller and the Testerman brothers watching the transaction. Their eyes widened at Legrand's stinginess. Then, they dropped their gaze to study their muddy shoes. She supposed the trio knew something unlucky would soon happen to Roderick Legrand.

The walk home from the corner lot to Drucilla's picket-fence bordered yard was short. Once inside her tidy cottage, Drucilla set Shadow on his favorite windowsill and opened the window.

"Let me know if anyone comes to the door," she instructed her pet.

Shadow mewed in response. Then, he turned his head and began to survey the quiet neighborhood.

Somewhat sorry she'd been pushed into using her witchy skills once more, Drucilla brought water to a boil in her favorite pan. Next, she added salt and a dead flower she'd plucked from the ground at Roderick Legrand's feet to the bubbling liquid. When steam rose from the pan like an angry ghost, she chanted a leaky roof curse.

A smile curling her lips, Drucilla carried the pan to the window and tossed the mixture into the summer air while repeating the leaky roof curse three more times.

"Let's see how many cloudbursts it takes before Roderick Legrand visits me," Drucilla Darkwander told her cat as she closed the window. Returning to the kitchen, she chuckled at the thought of rain leaking into the house the developer was building on the corner lot. When he came calling, she suspected Roderick would pay her more than a twenty-dollar bill to remove the curse.

Shadow meowed, hopped from the windowsill, padded across the living room, and rubbed against Drucilla's leg. Then he lifted his tar paper-black head and stared lovingly at her.

"No one cheats a Darkwander and gets away with it," said the water witch as she picked up Shadow and scratched his neck. "Magic shouldn't be needed to receive fair pay for a job well done." She kissed Shadow before adding, "But sometimes, magic *is* necessary."

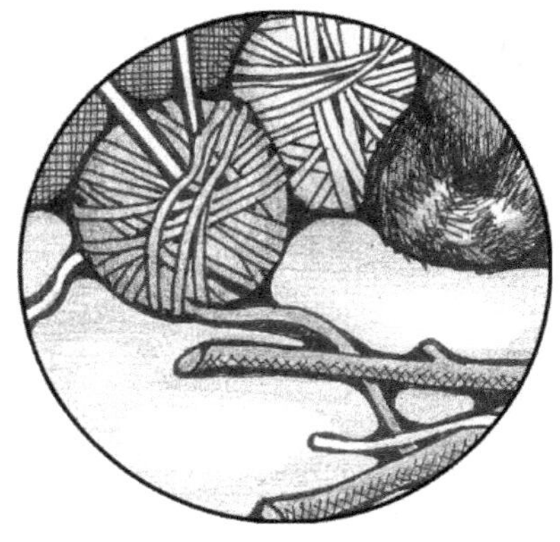

Mossy Bog

"...a scarcely perceptible creek, oozing its way through a wilderness of reeds and slime..."
– The Gold Bug

While visiting her Aunt Verds, Uncle Augustus, and cousin Gordon, Polly wanted to explore Mossy Bog. The bog's miles of swampy land and countless streams and ponds intrigued her. She wondered what creatures lived there and which plants grew between the cypress trees.

"Can we go down to Mossy Bog for a few minutes?" Polly asked as soon as her parents went inside her cousin's house.

"It's getting late," said Gordon. "We should wait and visit the bog tomorrow morning."

"Let's just take a quick look. Please," begged Polly. "Then, we can hurry back to your house for dinner."

"Okay," replied Gordon reluctantly. "But we can't still be in Mossy Bog at dusk."

The cousins strolled down the path toward the swamp lands. As they walked, Polly noticed the gnarled trees were draped with huge hunks of gray-green moss. She also noted the buzz of insects grew louder, the soil beneath her feet grew muddier, and the smell of decay grew stronger.

After stopping and studying the sky, Gordon said, "Time to head back."

"Why?" asked Polly. "There's plenty of daylight left."

"Maybe, maybe not," said Gordon. Her cousin dropped his voice to a whisper and added, "But we need to get out of here, because there's something evil in Mossy Bog."

"Evil! Seriously?" Polly snickered. "So, what does this *evil* look like?"

"It has scales," began her cousin.

"Like a water moccasin?" she asked.

"But it's not a snake." Gordon chewed on his fingernails before adding, "It has wide jaws."

"Like an alligator?" she asked.

"Yes, but it's not a gator." Still chewing on his fingernails, he scanned the marshy land around them. "And it has bulging eyes."

"Like a frog?" Polly was beginning to doubt her cousin's truthfulness.

"But it's not a frog," he answered. Gordon pulled on his lower lip. Eyes darting from one side of the path to the other, he whispered, "It has wings and wicked claws."

"Like a vulture?" said Polly.

"Yes, but it's *not* a vulture." Her cousin started walking backwards up the trail. "And it has fangs filled with venom."

"Like a spider?" she asked. Gordon's fear was beginning to creep her out. She peered into the nearby swamp looking for whatever had scales, wide jaws, bulging eyes, wings, wicked claws, and venomous fangs.

"Worse," replied her cousin. He took several more steps backward. "But it's not a spider. It's a bog beast."

"A bog beast!" Polly laughed. "That's the silliest thing I've ever heard."

"Shush," hissed Gordon. "Laughter lures Mossy."

"Mossy?" Polly was convinced her cousin had lost his mind. She wasn't about to buy into some ridiculous legend.

Polly was going to tell him as much when Gordon's eyes opened wide. Raising his left hand, he pointed at something behind her. His mouth opened and shut like he was trying to say something but had forgotten the words.

Suddenly, Gordon screamed, "Mossy! It's behind you!" before turning and racing up the path.*

"Sure." Polly was absolutely convinced her cousin was a major wimp. Just to make sure he was lying, she glanced over her shoulder.

Towering over her was a terrible beast. It had mud-covered scales, huge jaws, eyes nearly popping out of its warty face, leathery wings, claws as big as knives, and fangs dripping with what was surely venom.

"Mossy," whispered Polly just before the bog beast grabbed her.

*When you read this part, you can point at one of the listeners.

2024

Ravens

"...the silent flight of the raven-winged..."
– Berenice

Feathers blacker than a moonless night
fold neatly against your inky back.

Sharp beak harder than a rose's thorn
opens, closes as you tilt your head.

Two eyes brighter than a lightning strike
patiently observe a busy road.

Voice more raucous than a flight of crows
squawks a scavenger's dinnertime song.

Wings shinier than a polished skull
spread as you descend down to roadkill.

Then, claws sharper than a pitchfork's prongs
pierce the flesh of a shattered squirrel.

Bird brains cleverer than people know,
ravens roost in cemetery oaks.

Minds much older than ours see ahead:
fresh meals to be found among the dead.

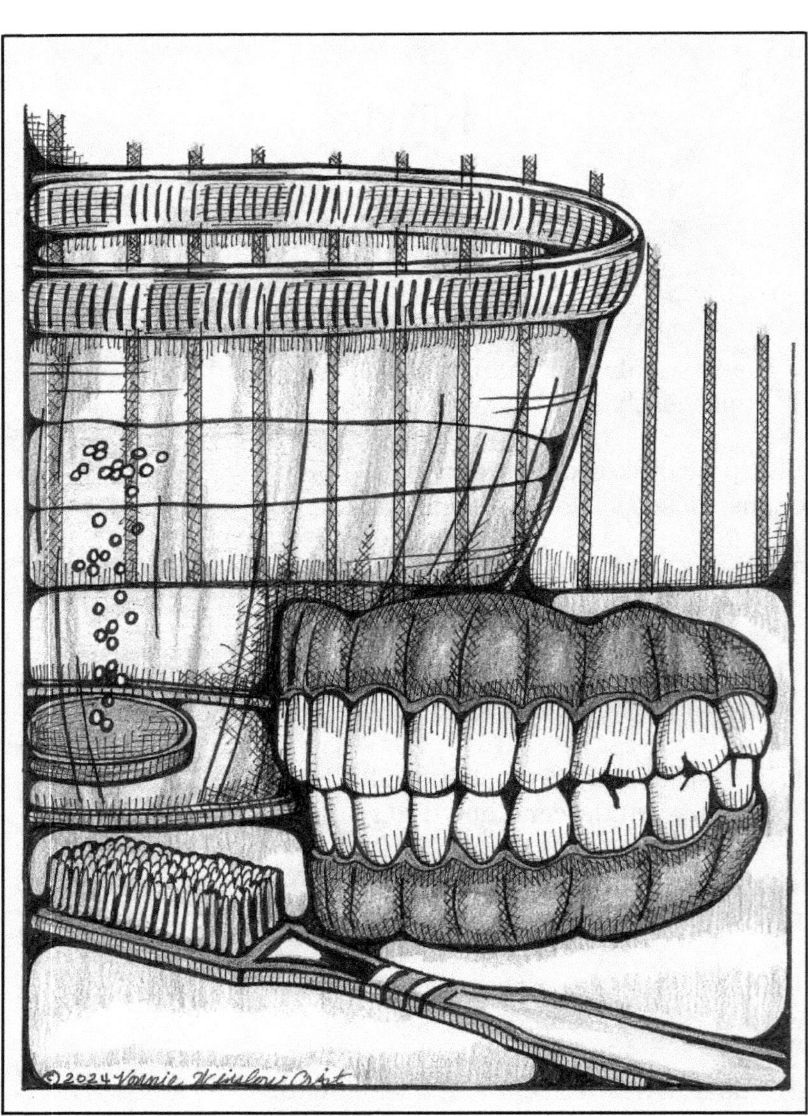
©2024 Vonnie Winslow Crist

Pop's Teeth

"...the most entirely even, and the most brilliantly white of all conceivable teeth."
– The Man That Was Used Up

Bella peeked around the door frame. Pop's dentures smiled at her from a cup of water sitting on the nightstand beside his bed.

After glancing down the hall to make certain she was alone, Bella stepped into Pop's bedroom. She felt her heart thumping faster than her grandfather's teeth clicked together when he ate dinner. She took seven more steps into the room. Tilting her head slightly, she studied the two gleaming rows of teeth glued onto pretend pink gums. At least, she assumed they were glued on.

Her grandfather's dentures had always fascinated Bella. She supposed it was because Pop took them out each night and pushed them into place each morning. During the hours in between, the smiling dentures rested in their glass of water.

As far as she knew, everyone else in her family and all her friends, except Nico Curtis, had real teeth. Bella had learned about Nico's false teeth by accident. When they were in fifth grade, she had complimented him on the whiteness of his front teeth.

Nico had laughed.

"Six of my teeth were knocked out when I was playing hockey." He tapped his incisors. "The dentist made these and screwed them into my jawbone."

"Cool," Bella had answered. Though the whole hockey accident, dentist visit, and screwed in teeth sounded painful.

Thoughts of Nico's replacement teeth vanished when Bella spotted movement in the cup of water where Pop's teeth soaked. She narrowed her eyes and observed the submerged dentures. As she watched, a string of teeny bubbles rose to the top of the water. She sighed. The movement she'd noticed a few seconds earlier was probably bubbles. Every night before he went to sleep, she knew her grandfather dropped a fizzy tablet into the denture water to clean his teeth. A few leftover bubbles made sense.

After looking over her shoulder once more, Bella tiptoed closer to the nightstand. She gazed down into the cup holding Pop's teeth. The view from above was clearer. The sides of the glass container were curved, so they distorted the dentures' shape and dimmed their colors. Looking down, the pinkness of the gums and whiteness of the teeth were more vivid.

She ran the tip of her tongue across the tops of her own teeth. Then, pressing her lips together, Bella touched the cup's rim with the forefinger of her right hand.

So far, so good, she thought.

Next, she dipped her finger into the water.

It's colder than I thought it would be, she mused.

Summoning her courage, Bella pushed her fingers deeper into the water. She touched the edge of the false gums. They were surprisingly smooth. She tapped the surface of one top tooth. The clicking of her fingernail against the cuspid sounded loud in the quiet bedroom. Finally, she stuck her fingers between the upper and lower dentures.

*Snap!**

Like a sprung trap, the teeth clamped down on the fingers of her right hand.

Calling for help, she jumped back and tried to shake the dentures from her fingers. But the teeth held on.

"Help," she shouted as she ran to the bedroom door with Pop's teeth dangling from her fingers.

The teeth began to grind. Blood dripped down her hand.

"Pop!" she hollered as she raced down the hall.

"Bella," he answered. "I'm coming."

But as she heard Pop's teeth grinding against bone, she doubted her grandfather would arrive in time to save her fingers.

It's a good thing I'm left-handed, Bella thought before she blacked out from the pain.

*You can clap your hands loudly one time as you say, "Snap!"

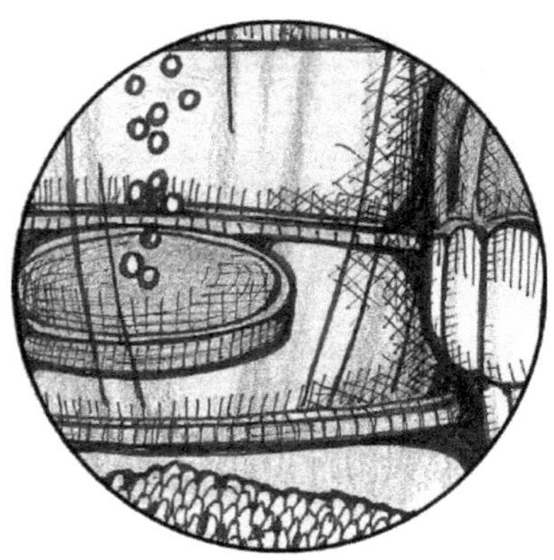

Mid-Eclipse

"...the moon arose through the thin ghastly mist, and it was crimson in color."
– Silence – A Fable

Dying to watch the moon turn red, John decided to sleep in his clothes so he could quickly jump out of bed and view the moon. Before he fell asleep, he set his alarm for mid-eclipse. But his dog's howls woke him before the alarm sounded.

"What's wrong, Gruff?" he asked her.

Gruff dashed to the glass door that led to their side yard. Her tail drooped as she stood there gazing at the moon. She lifted her chin and howled again in a mournful voice.

"It's just an eclipse," John told his dog as he knelt beside her. He scratched her neck and stared out the glass door at the blood-colored moon. "Nothing to worry about."

No sooner had he spoken than he spotted a dark, wolfish shape racing across his neighbors' yards toward the glass door. The skin on the back of his neck prickled as a terrible howling came from the creature.

Not waiting for the beast to draw closer, Gruff scrambled for cover. But John found he couldn't move.

Moments later, an enormous wolf man stood on the other side of the door. Back lit by the eclipsed moon, the snarling beast glared at him with emerald eyes.

John possessed no silver bullets or silver dagger to dispatch the werewolf. Still frozen in place, he awaited breaking glass and sharp teeth.

©2024

It Tickles

"...like the thread of the spider..."
– The Tell-Tale Heart

It was a steamy July afternoon. The breeze ruffling the boxwoods beside Uncle Bransby's porch felt cool against Lily's skin. The wind also swayed the porch's hammock and rocked Lily to sleep.

When she awoke from her nap, Lily felt a tickling in her ear. She sat up, swung her legs to the side of the hammock, and shook her head. Still, the tickling continued.

Next, she pulled her hair into a ponytail and tied it with a rubber band. But the tickling sensation did not go away.

Then, she yawned. Her ear didn't pop, and the tickling didn't stop.

Lily sighed. Whatever was causing the tickle was still there. So, she poked her fingertip in her ear, ran it around, then pulled it out. Looking down at her fingernail, she saw no wax, no stray cat hair, no tiny leaf.

Believing the annoying ear tickle was getting worse, she went into the house.

"Uncle Bransby," she called. "I think I've got something in my ear."

"Let me see," replied her uncle as he set down the book he was reading. After leaning close and looking into her ear, he grunted, then said, "I don't see anything. Probably somebody is talking about you. That's what makes your ears itch."

Lily giggled. "I think that's an old wives' tale," she told her uncle.

He peered over his glasses at her and winked. "Maybe so," he replied. "But drinking a glass of water sometimes helps."

That sounded like a reasonable idea. So, Lily went into the kitchen and got a drink of water.

It didn't help.

For the rest of the day and through the evening, she felt a tickling in her ear. She pressed on her face where her ear began. She rubbed the outside of her ear. She yawned and shook her head. Nothing helped. Finally, Lily did her best to ignore the weird feeling. At bedtime, she drank a glass of hot cocoa and eventually fell asleep.

***

In the morning, the tickling in Lily's ear was even worse. She went to the bathroom and gazed into the mirror to see if she could figure out what was irritating her ear.

"Oh, no," she gasped when she saw webbing covering her ear.

Quickly, Lily brushed the sticky threads away. But what was underneath was even more horrible. Hundreds of baby spiders raced out of the ear canal. Some crept into her hair. Some crawled across her face. Some dropped down onto her shoulders.

"Help!" she screamed as she ran toward her uncle. "A spider laid its eggs in my ear and they're hatching!"

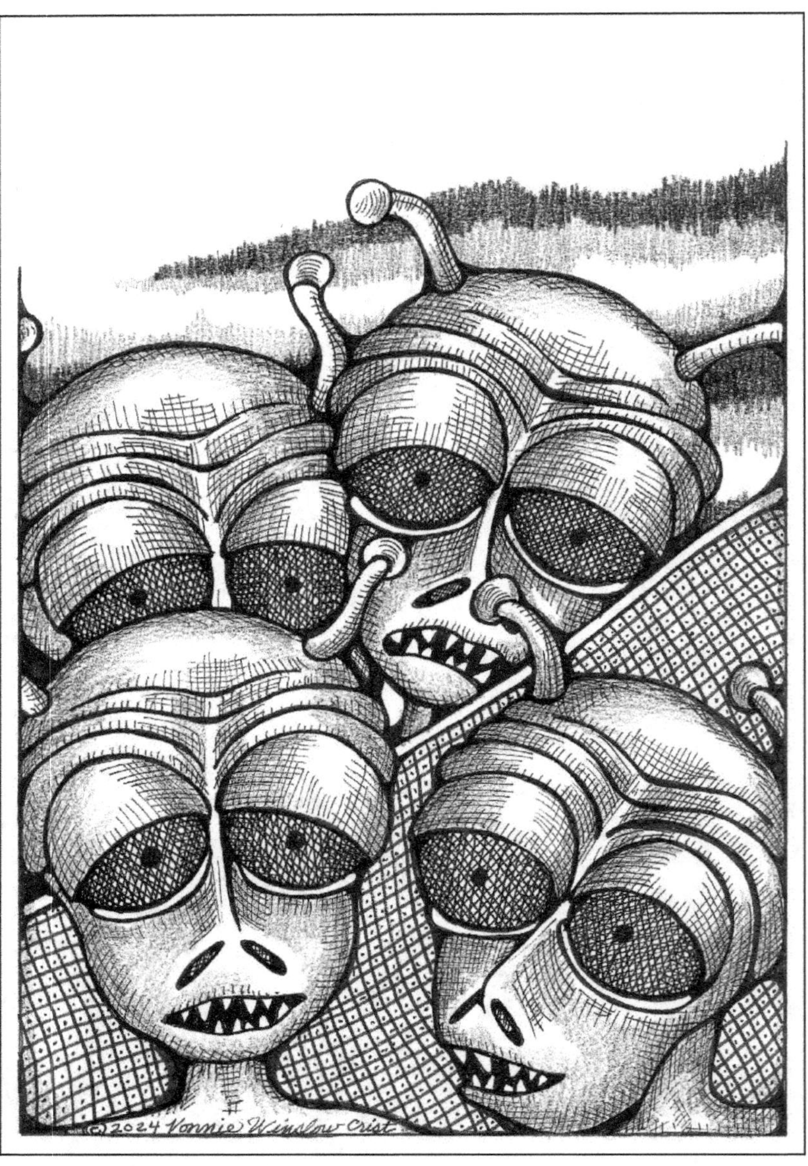
©2024 Vonnie Winslow Crist

Northern Lights

"...all terrestrial objects immediately around us, were glowing in the unnatural light..."
– The Fall of the House of Usher

Standing in the vacant lot next to their family's townhouse, Hans and Bobby Tompkins gazed up at the stars.

"I don't see anything," said Bobby. "Maybe there weren't really disturbances on the sun sending solar winds toward earth."

"Be patient," Hans told him. "We *should* be able to see the aurora borealis tonight."

Bobby glanced at his older brother. Hans always seemed so sure of himself.

"I need to finish my homework," he said. "I'm going back inside. Give me a yell if you see the northern lights."

"Wait!" Hans pointed up. "Look!"

"The sky is shimmering pinkish red and spring green!" exclaimed Bobby. "I guess the solar winds *did* reach the upper atmosphere."

"Pretty amazing," Hans replied. "Now, aren't you glad you came outside with—"

"What's that?" interrupted Bobby. He grabbed his brother's upper arm and pointed at the playground across the street.

An eerie lime-colored glow lit the swings, slides, and climbing wall.

"Let's go see." Hans hurried across the empty street.

Not wanting to be left behind, Bobby followed.

Seconds later, he spotted about twenty short, gray-skinned men standing in the greenish light. They turned their huge, black eyes in the direction of Hans and him.

"Aliens," he whispered.

"Run," screamed Hans as the aliens rushed in their direction carrying shimmering nets.

Bobby heard a whistling sound. Out of the corner of his eye, he saw Hans fall to the ground as he was caught in a net.

"Keep running," shouted his brother.

Unfortunately, Bobby had to stop at the edge of their street to avoid getting hit by a passing car. Before he could cross the road, he heard the whistling of an alien net. When the net touched him, Bobby felt an electrical shock. Then, he fell to the ground.

"Got you!"* hissed a group of the gray-skinned beings as they grabbed him. Then the aliens carried Bobby to their vessel.

At least I'm not alone, he thought as the spaceship rose into the night air. For across from him tangled in the aliens' nets, Bobby saw not only Hans, but four other kids from their neighborhood.

*If you are reading this story to someone else, you can grab their arm when you say this.

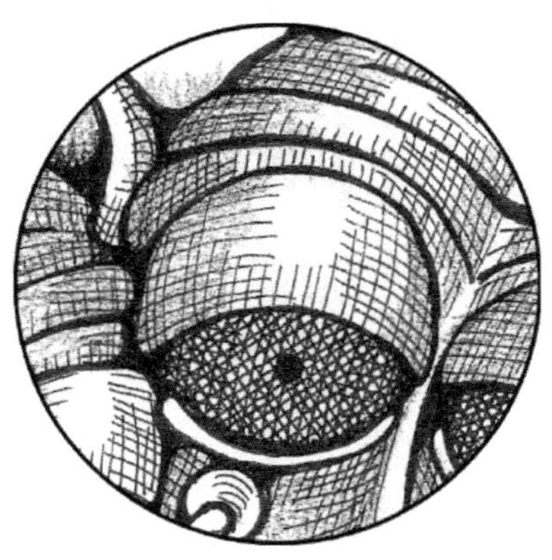

Vonnie Crist ©

Swimming Alone

"So lovely was the loneliness. Of a wild lake..."
– The Lake

After jogging all the way from the parking lot to Blackwood Lake, perspiration dampened Mary's back. Annie, Helen, and Elizabeth had chosen to walk the lake trail. Therefore, they were a few minutes behind her. Rather than wait for her friends to arrive, Mary decided to swim alone.

She sat on a mossy rock by the edge of the lake. Having worn a bathing suit under her clothing, it only took a few minutes to remove her shoes, socks, shorts, and t-shirt. Folding her clothes carefully, Mary placed them on top of the towel she'd carried with her on her jog. Since it fit tightly, she decided to leave on her silver ring with a naturally shaped turquoise stone set in the center.

Then, she stood, took a couple of steps forward, and surveyed the shoreline. No one else was around.

Cupping her right hand over her eyes to shield them from the sunlight reflected by the water, she scanned the far shore of the small Blackwood Lake inlet. No other swimmers were visible.

"Wow! It sure is quiet here," she said.

A small splash and the hum of a bee answered her.

Laughing at her sudden case of nerves, Mary waded into the cool, dark water.

"Annie, Helen, and Elizabeth will be here soon," she told

the dragonflies flitting nearby. "So there is no need to worry."

Out of the corner of her eye, Mary noticed bubbles bursting on the surface a few meters away. She wondered what sort of fish created them.

Suddenly, a horse's head lifted from the water.

Mary screamed.

The horse didn't flinch. Instead, it leaned its beautifully formed head toward her and whinnied.

Though she thought the soft whinny sounded like the animal was friendly, Mary shook her head.

"No," she whispered.

With a coat as brown as the hemlock-stained water, the horse seemed to be a part of Blackwood Lake rather than an animal swimming in its waters. Knowing it had her attention, the horse blew air from its nostrils. Mary saw a stream of bubbles dripping from its nose.

"So, that's where the bubbles came from," she said. "Not a fish, but a water horse."

As she said the words *water horse*, the beast nodded its head. It gazed at her with pale eyes that begged Mary to paddle closer. Knowing better, but drawn to the lovely, brown animal, she swam toward it.

When Mary finally drew alongside the water horse, the urge to ride the animal was overwhelming.

Just a short ride, she thought as she climbed aboard the horse. Once she was astride the beast, it plowed through the water at an alarming speed. But it didn't head across the inlet. Rather, the water horse swam toward the larger, deeper part of Blackwood Lake.

"Stop!" hollered Mary as she struggled to climb from the animal's back. But she discovered she could not dismount.

Just as the beast plunged to the lake's bottom with Mary still on its back, she remembered the proper name for a water horse.

Kelpie! she thought. *I'm riding a kelpie.*

Her lungs threatening to burst from holding her breath too long under water, Mary knew she was close to passing out. As she slipped into unconsciousness, one last thought floated in her mind, *I'm doomed. Kelpies drown and devour their riders.*

***

"Hey!" said Elizabeth pointing to some clothes stacked on a rock. "Aren't those Mary's things?"

"I think so," answered Annie. "And those shoes are definitely hers."

The three girls looked around. Smooth as glass, the tea-colored water shone brightly. But Mary was nowhere to be seen.

"Maybe she headed back to the parking lot," suggested Helen.

"We would have seen her on the path," said Elizabeth.

"Look!" whispered Annie. "What's that on the shore?"

The three friends stepped closer. They stared at a severed finger, laying at the water's edge. On the finger was a silver ring with a naturally shaped turquoise stone set in the center.

And then, they screamed.

© 2024
Vonnie Winslow Crist

Black Dog

"...panting after him, with open mouth and glaring eyes, there darted a huge beast."
– A Tale of the Ragged Mountain

Walking home from his best friend Andy's house, Thomas heard the distant cry of a hound. Slightly unnerved, he increased his pace.

"I should have listened to Mom and headed home before dark," he said. Thomas glanced around. The sidewalks were empty except for a black cat scratching a fence post two yards further down the street. The cat glared at Thomas with yellow eyes. Then it darted across the walk in front of him.

Knowing it was bad luck when a black cat crossed your path, Thomas reached into his pocket. He pulled out the penny he had found this afternoon. When he'd spotted the penny, Andy and he had said together, "See a penny and pick it up. All day long you'll have good luck." Thomas hoped the penny was still working.

As he slipped the copper coin back into his pants' pocket, the unseen dog howled once more. This time, the canine sounded much closer.

Mr. Lyttleton, who sat on a bench in front of the barbershop all day, had warned Thomas, Andy, and anyone else who would listen about Black Dog. Mr. Lyttleton said Black Dog roamed the town at night looking for disobedient kids. He'd explained when the otherworldly canine spied a kid, it chased them. Next, the old man had told Thomas that sometimes Black Dog allowed people to make it home alive. After shaking his head, Mr. Lyttleton had lowered his voice and whispered, "But often, naughty kids are never seen again."

Perhaps someone is hunting with their dog, Thomas thought. But hunting or not, the crying dog gave Thomas goosebumps. He felt certain he needed to get home as soon as possible. So, pulse racing, he began to run.

The melancholy baying grew louder. Thomas looked over his shoulder at the road behind him. He swallowed a scream when he saw a huge dog loping after him. Maybe it was nothing more than the streetlights' reflection, but the canine's eyes and exposed fangs appeared to glow. Thomas was certain it was Black Dog.

Still thinking about Mr. Lyttleton's warning, Thomas turned the corner. His house was at the end of the block. Running now as fast as his feet would carry him, Thomas hoped he could reach home before Black Dog caught him. About halfway down the block, he heard his lucky penny clinking as it bounced out of his pocket and hit the pavement.

Then Thomas heard the pad of Black Dog's paws on the concrete and felt its hot breath on the back of his neck. He opened his mouth to call for his mom. But before he could shout her name, Black Dog's jaws clamped onto his shoulder.

As he was dragged into the shadows by the frightening hound, Thomas knew his good luck had rolled away.

REST
IN
PEACE
Remember Me
©2024 Vonnie Winslow Crist

Bells

"Oh, the bells, bells, bells! What a tale their terror tells..."
– The Bells

On a warm August evening, Tommy Dobson and his sisters, Ginny and Violet, hosted a hot dog roast in their backyard. They each invited two friends.

Mom and Dad watched everyone put their hot dogs onto the roasting sticks and cook them over the campfire. Once the wieners were done, they helped Tommy, Ginny, Violet, and their friends take them off the sticks and slide them into buns.

Afterwards, Mom brought out marshmallows, graham crackers, and chocolate bars for s'mores. When all nine kids couldn't eat another mouthful, Tommy's parents carried the leftovers into the house.

Finally alone, the friends sat on logs around the fire.

"Let's tell ghost stories," said Ginny.

Her suggestion was met with screams of "Yes!"

"You start, Tommy," suggested Violet. "You're good at telling stories."

"Okay," agreed Tommy.

His sisters and their friends fell silent and waited for him to begin.

"Before doctors had better tests, when someone died, they'd stick a mirror under the person's nose. If no breath caused the mirror to fog up, then the patient was declared dead," began Tommy.

He could tell by the way everyone was leaning forward that they were listening. So, he continued.

"But this isn't a reliable way to determine if a person is dead. So, lots of people were buried alive."

A chorus of "Oh, no," No way," and "Seriously?" followed.

"Seriously," he assured everyone. "It was so bad, that when a person was buried, the undertaker would tie a string around the body's wrist. The string ran out of the coffin, up through the ground, and was attached to a bell. If the supposedly dead person woke up, they would pull on the string and ring the bell. Then, the undertaker would dig the coffin back up and save the person from smothering."

"Is that true?" asked Ginny.

"Yup," he told his sister. "But it gets worse."

Again, Tommy noticed everyone leaned closer.

"Sometimes, the undertaker fell asleep or was on the other side of the cemetery when a person who'd been buried alive woke up. And he didn't hear the bell."

Tommy shrugged his shoulders before adding, "So that person would scream, claw at the top of the coffin, and ring the bell until they finally smothered."

A chorus of "Gross," "That's awful," and "I don't believe you" erupted from his listeners.

"You don't *have* to believe me," said Tommy. "Look it up tomorrow. Oh, and I forgot to tell you, there's an abandoned cemetery just over that hill."

He pointed to the slope which rose from the Dobson family's backyard to a fenced-off area. Before Tommy could share any more details, the sound of bells ringing came from the direction of the old cemetery.*

Eight kids yelled for Mr. and Mrs. Dobson and raced into the house.

Tommy looked up the hill. He wondered if he should grab a shovel, search for bells tied to strings, and dig up a grave or two.

*If you are reading this story to someone, you can ring a bell when you read this sentence.

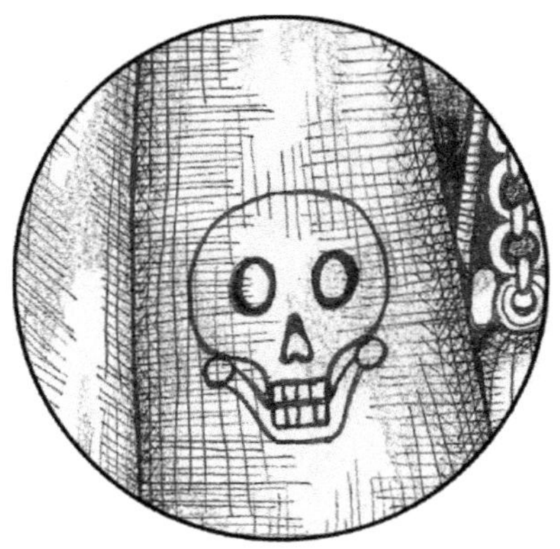

© Vonnie Winslow Crist

Gargoyles in the Garden

"In the most enchanting of natural landscapes, there will always be found a defect..."
– The Landscape Garden

Though it was twilight, Charley spotted Miss Pennifeather, the school librarian, still working in her garden.

"Miss Penni, isn't it a little late to be pulling weeds?" Charley called to her neighbor.

After straightening up and brushing back some curls that had fallen into her face, Miss Penni motioned for Charley to come over.

"I wanted to watch my night bloomers open," explained the librarian. She brushed her fingers across a bushy plant covered in ruffly, five-petaled blossoms. "The four o'clocks have already bloomed." Then she pointed to a mass of vines with heart-shaped leaves beside a dragonish statue. "The moonflowers will be opening soon."

"Moonflowers? I thought plants needed sunlight," said Charley. As she waited for the librarian's answer, she rubbed the wrinkled forehead of a nearby cement statue with hooved feet and a long snout. It was the closest of the two dozen or so gargoyle statues that dotted Miss Penni's garden. Years ago, Charley had asked the librarian why she had so many gargoyles. Her neighbor explained that the ugly-looking beasts were used for protection. She said for hundreds of years, people have believed gargoyles keep evil away. Then, she'd added, "And there's something charming about their wrinkly, toothy faces and scaly, misshapen bodies."

A pale green moth floating by Charley's shoulder interrupted her thoughts. She refocused on the librarian and her flowers.

"Night bloomers *do* need sun," said Miss Penni. "But they flower after sundown. So, instead of being pollinated by bees and butterflies, the plants in my moon garden are pollinated by bats, fireflies, and moths. Just like that luna moth." Her neighbor pointed at the moth that had flown by Charley.

Charley bent down and sniffed the four o'clocks. "They smell amazing."

"They do have a lovely scent. Though, I suspect you're also smelling the sweet alyssum." With the toe of her shoe, the librarian touched a mass of delicate, white flowers covering the ground at the foot of the four o'clocks and spilling onto the sidewalk.

Before she could ask any more questions, Charley spotted movement at the rear of the garden where its neatly trimmed shrubs met the edge of the forest. She took a step in the direction of the woods and strained to see what was skulking in its shadows.

"Miss Penni," she whispered, "I think there's someone hiding in the woods."

Her neighbor moved to stand beside Charley. She stared into the dark thicket of trees.

Suddenly, an enormous, shaggy creature strode out of the forest. It towered ten or eleven feet high. From the top of its head sprouted ferns, grasses, and mushrooms. Beneath two bushy eyebrows drawn down in a horrible frown glowed one huge eye. Charley didn't want to imagine what had happened to the missing eye.

"Skogtroll!" exclaimed Miss Penni as she pushed Charley behind her. "Don't run," she ordered. "If we stand still, the skogtroll might ignore us and go about its business."

"What business could it have here?" asked Charley as quietly as possible.

At the sound of her hushed voice, the troll turned its face in their direction and sniffed.

"Fresh meats," growled the creature. "Old or young. They'll taste sweet going down."

When the skogtroll spoke, Charley saw below its drooping mustache and above its scraggly beard, the creature's mouth was filled with sharp teeth. After moistening its lips with a thick tongue, the skogtroll patted its stomach and walked toward Miss Penni and her.

"No meats here," said the librarian. "Only trouble."

The troll chuckled. It raised its four-fingered hands and reached forward as if to grab Miss Penni.

A chorus of snarls, growls, and yelps burst from the gargoyles. In the blink of an eye, the concrete statues came to life. Hooves clattered, claws slashed, wings flapped, tails whipped, and jaws snapped as Miss Penni's garden gargoyles attacked the skogtroll.

As the horde continued their assault, the troll's gleaming eye widened.

"Too much trouble," grumbled the creature. Knocking the last angry gargoyle from its shoulder, the skogtroll turned and lumbered back into the forest. Apparently, it had no desire to battle twenty-some biting, clawing statues that had come to life.

The gargoyles kept up their snarling and howling until the skogtroll had disappeared into the depths of the woods. Then, one by one, the grotesque beasts came to the librarian. She patted each bumpy head, scratched under each scaled chin, then thanked each of her garden statues. Once the gargoyles had returned to their assigned places in the garden, Miss Penni wrapped her arm around Charley's shoulder.

"Thank you again, my pets," said Miss Pennifeather in a voice quite loud for a librarian. "Charley and I are grateful for your protection."

"Yes. Thanks," added Charley. Still shocked by the appearance of a skogtroll, the animation of the statues, and the parade of gargoyles looking for pats and scratches, she could think of nothing more to say. Instead, she studied the face of her neighbor.

Moonlight caught in Miss Pennifeather's eyes. They seemed to sparkle with a magical glimmer as she told the stone-gray beasts, "Back to sleep, my lovelies."

As suddenly as they'd come alive, two dozen gargoyles froze.

Before Charley could ask one of the many questions whirling around in her mind, Miss Penni pressed her forefinger to her lips and made a shushing sound.

"Go home, Charley," the librarian told her. "Tonight's events *must* remain a secret. Do you understand?"

"I understand," she replied.

Then, Miss Penni handed her a moonflower blossom. "Put this under your pillow for sweet dreams. If you'd like to know more about skogtrolls and their kin, come see me in the morning. I have a book you can borrow."

Charley nodded. Before she hurried down the sidewalk toward her house, she bent down and picked up a claw which must have broken off a gargoyle's paw when it attacked the troll. Clutching the claw in one hand and the moonflower in the other, Charley looked back at Miss Penni. Her neighbor was sweeping up the broken plant parts that littered her garden's walkways after the troll-gargoyle fight.

It occurred to her: The librarian's broom wasn't the store-bought kind. Instead, Miss Pennifeather's broom looked like the ones used by witches to fly, Baba Yaga to sweep away her tracks, and the old woman who was tossed ninety times as high as the moon to clean the cobwebs from the sky.

Was Miss Penni a witch or magic-wielder or both? Charley wasn't certain. But as she felt the sharp point of a gargoyle's claw in her hand, she *was* certain she'd keep her promise to never tell a living soul about the skogtroll and gargoyles.

For the consequences of sharing Miss Pennifeather's secrets might be terrible indeed!

© 2024

Giggles

"Ha! ha! ha!—he! he! he!—a very good joke indeed—an excellent jest."
– The Cask of Amontillado

Joel had been afraid of clowns for as long as he could remember.

Unfortunately, Mr. Pym, the neighbor directly across the street from Joel's home, was a part-time clown named Giggles. People hired Giggles to appear at birthday parties. Joel refused to go to parties with a clown. People hired Giggles to march in the local parades. Joel would turn his head when he heard Giggles's clown horn. Its unmistakable *awooga-awooga-awooga* sound warned of the approaching white-faced, orange-haired, big-shoed, horrifying clown.

But Giggles living in Joel's neighborhood was the worst part.

Giggles thought it was funny to sneak up on the neighbor children. He would honk his *awooga* horn or pop a balloon or shout, "Boo!" Then, after the kids screamed, he'd giggle and hand them a piece of candy.

Most of the children laughed. "Good one, Mr. Pym," or, "Got me, Giggles," they'd say.

Not Joel. With his heart pounding and breath caught in his throat, he'd run home, go in the house, and slam the door. Joel wouldn't go outside for the rest of the day. He was afraid Giggles would be waiting for him.

Later, when he saw his neighbor in his yard watering the garden, Mr. Pym would say, "I'll make you laugh sooner or later, Joel. Just you wait and see."

He would shake his head and tell Mr. Pym, "I don't think so. To me, clowns aren't funny."

As the years went by, Giggles continued to frighten children and teens. And as the years went by, after he'd scared the neighbor kids, they'd accept the offered candy and laugh. All of them except Joel. Joel refused to laugh at the clown or take his candy.

One sweltering summer day, the news of Mr. Pym's death spread through the neighborhood like wildfire. Mr. Pym had died in his clown suit while performing at a retirement party. Although Joel was sorry his neighbor was gone, he was also relieved he wouldn't have to see a clown almost every day.

That night, Joel heard a tap on his window. He looked up but saw nothing. The next morning, he went outside and studied the soil in the garden under his bedroom window. There were huge footprints in the soft earth.

They look like clown shoe footprints, he thought. The skin on the back of his neck prickled.

The next night, Joel heard a loud pop. When he glanced over at the window, he saw a red balloon floating on the other side of the glass. In the morning, he hurried outside and found five partially deflated balloons on the ground below his window.

They look like the balloons Giggles used to carry, he thought. A chill tingled his spine.

On the third night, Joel went to bed late. He didn't want to be in his room alone, but he was too old for spooky fears. Once he was under the covers and the lights were out, he heard the crinkling noise of someone unwrapping candy.

"Giggles?" said Joel in a quivering voice.

"Yes."

Joel started to shake. He heard a floppy shoe scrape against the floor at the foot of his bed.

"Why are you here?" he asked.

"You know why," came the answer from the shadows.

Joel sat up. He pulled the covers up to his chin.

"I *don't* know why," he replied.

"To make you laugh!"

Out of the shadows jumped Giggles. Dressed in his yellow overalls with a blue and purple striped shirt underneath, the clown waved his white-gloved hands on either side of his face. Though Giggles's orange hair still sprouted from either side of his balding head, his face had changed. He had an eye where his mouth ought to be, an ear where an eyebrow should be, and his big, red nose was stuck to the side of his head. The clown's exaggerated mouth smiled upside down on his forehead, while the second ear dangled from his chin like a strange beard.

Even though he was scared, the clown's face looked so weird that Joel laughed.

"Got you!" said Giggles with a hollow giggle. Then, in the wink of an eye, the clown's face returned to its normal appearance. He touched his forehead with the fingers of his right glove, nodded, then vanished.

Terrified, Joel turned on the light beside his bed.

"Whew! That was some nightmare," he told himself. And he believed it. Until he saw a handful of candy, a red balloon, and a few strands of orange hair laying on the bedspread at the end of his bed.

Vonnie Winslow Crist
© 2024

Watching

"...a dragon of a scaly and prodigious demeanor, and of a fiery tongue, which sate in guard..."
– The Fall of the House of Usher

On foggy mornings, when it's damp
and a chilly rain drizzles down,
they nap in your basement,
waiting for your footfalls on the stairs.

When you walk in the forest,
a canopy of green spreading overhead,
they dangle from tree limbs,
memorizing your scent.

During the middle of the afternoon,
when the day is at its hottest,
they curl in the shade humming along
as you sing a childhood tune.

On blustery days, when you check
for split trees and fallen branches,
they nestle beneath the evergreens,
studying your every move.

In the autumn, when deer count on
ground apples, acorns, and leftover corn,
they hunker down between the pumpkins
wondering if you'll share.

Before each holiday and festive gathering,
as you search for decorations,
they drape from attic rafters
learning your face.

When snow piles against the house
and you trudge outside to feed the birds,
they perch on the roof,
contemplating your kindness.

On melancholy afternoons, as you sort
through mementos of those now gone,
they lean over your shoulder
observing your sorrow.

In the evening, as the stars blink to life
and you read your favorite book,
they stretch behind the sofa,
counting the pages as you turn them.

Late at night, as you close your eyes,
pull up the covers, and fall asleep,
they emerge from the darkness intent on
scrutinizing your dreams.

When you slumber, awash in moonbeams,
they hide beneath your bed
among forgotten socks, shoes, and dust,
listening to you breathe.

So, know,
no matter the year, time, or season,
whenever you sense something staring,
hear the swoosh of scales sliding,

feel the back of your neck prickling,
and realize you are not alone—
dragons are near and watching.
For dragons are *always* watching.

©2024

Crickets

"...It is merely a cricket which has made a single chirp."
– The Tell-Tale Heart

"There is going to be a killing frost tonight," said Mom as she slipped on her plaid jacket. "Which means I need your help in the garden, Miranda."

"You know I hate gardening," whined Randi. "Can't you do it?"

Her mother shook her head. "No. Every tomato needs to be plucked off the vine. Then after bringing them inside, we need to wrap each unripe one in newspaper. Luckily," Mom smiled before continuing, "we only need to pick the green peppers and beans. No newspapers involved."

Randi groaned. Why did her mother have to be so cheerful about work? Resigned to help clear the vegetable garden of usable produce, Randi pulled on her navy fleece. Then she followed Mom outside.

The September air had a bite to it. Even without the weather forecaster's warning, Randi felt the coldness rushing down from the north.

"You work on the tomatoes while I pick the beans," said her mother as she handed Randi a half-bushel basket.

"Fine," grumbled Randi.

"Remember to pick the green ones, too, if they're bigger than a marble. We'll sort them out inside," said Mom.

Randi didn't answer. Instead, she began gently tugging tomatoes from the vines, even the larger green ones, and placing them in her basket. She had only picked three tomatoes when a huge, black cricket jumped on her arm.

"Eek!" she screamed. After looking at her for an instant with its compound eyes, the cricket hopped back into the tomato vines. Whether she had frightened the insect or if it had planned to leap off her sleeve all along, she didn't know.

Randi shivered. Not a fan of insects in general, and especially crickets, she had researched them. Her father always said, "It's best to know your enemy." While not exactly an enemy, in Randi's mind crickets and their kin were definitely unfriendly acquaintances.

Mom peeked from behind the pole beans. "Everything okay?" she asked.

"Yes. Just a cricket," answered Randi.

"Don't worry about them," replied her mother. "They don't bite. They're only here for the veggies."

"Actually, some crickets *do* bite," she responded under her breath. Obviously, Mom hadn't read as much about crickets as Randi.

Lost in picking beans, Mom hummed a song Randi didn't recognize.

She shook her head. She did *not* know why her mother had to hum all the time. It really annoyed Randi. Doing her best to ignore Mom's humming, she went back to picking tomatoes.

Her basket was nearly full by the time her mother had picked the peppers and beans. Randi was happy when Mom moved to the tomato patch. With both of them gathering tomatoes, it only took five more minutes to finish.

"A stack of old newspapers is waiting for you on the table," said Mom as she walked toward the kitchen door. "It shouldn't take long to wrap the green ones."

Randi groaned. Lugging her basket filled with ripened and unripened tomatoes, she followed her mother. When she stepped inside, the air in the kitchen was warm and smelled like fresh basil.

Mom set her basket down on the floor beside the sink.

Immediately she began placing the ripe tomatoes on the counter.

As Randi took off her fleece, she glanced at the newspapers stacked in the center of the kitchen table. Beside the newspapers was a cardboard box. After she wrapped each green tomato, Randi would place them in the box. Over the next few days, maybe even weeks, the tomatoes would ripen. As they turned red, her mother would use them in cooking.

Randi knew gardening saved money. She knew it was healthier to eat fresh vegetables. But she still wasn't a fan of the creepy crawlies that lived among the plants.

Today, the garden had been filled with crickets. They had been singing louder than usual. She supposed the crickets knew that tonight a killing frost would silence their songs. Though thanks to her research, Randi knew they weren't actually singing. The chirping sound coming from them was made by their legs, not their throats.

A cheep from beside the refrigerator interrupted her thoughts. She looked in the direction of the noise. A fat, black cricket stared back at her. It moved its antenna, then hopped in her direction.

Dropping the tomato she was wrapping, Randi took a couple of steps and raised her foot.

"Miranda, don't!" cried her mother.

But it was too late. Randi's shoe was already descending on the cricket. With a sickening pop, she stomped on and squished the long-legged insect.

"Bad luck," muttered Mom as she shook her head. "You should have let me catch the cricket and carry it outside."

"Nobody believes that bad luck stuff anymore," said Randi.

She scooped up the cricket's flattened remains with a scrap of newspaper. Then she took the dead cricket to the trash can. As she neared the can, Randi slipped on some tomato juice. She fell backwards with her left ankle beneath her. When she landed, a loud crack rang through the room and a sharp pain shot up her leg.

Fighting back tears, she saw the cricket's squashed body had fallen off the piece of newspaper she'd been carrying. Maybe it was her imagination, but the dead cricket's mouth seemed to smile. And despite being a fan of science and facts, Randi knew she'd have bad luck for the next seven years.

Vonnie Winslow Crist
©2024

Looking for Daniel O'Connell

"...the peculiar smell of decayed fungus arose to my nostrils."
– The Pit and the Pendulum

While Fletcher O'Connell's family was visiting with his great-aunt, great-uncle, and several dozen cousins, he'd decided to hike to the nearby cemetery. Supposedly, a few long-dead relatives were buried here, including the pirate, Captain Daring Dan O'Connell. He thought it would be cool to find Daniel O'Connell's grave. Plus, he didn't feel like chatting with a crowd of distant relations.

Fletch strolled through the abandoned cemetery. Landward gales kept its encircling stone wall, chiseled monuments, and brick walkways damp. As a result, they were encrusted with lichen and moss.

Fletch noticed windblown leaves had gathered in the corners of the burial yard and beside the bases of the markers. He also noted a variety of mushrooms etched a bright path across the sunken graves.

Perhaps, the frequent rain and constant mists that drift in on the ocean breezes have caused the burial plots to sink, he thought.

A chilly gust ruffled his hair.

And the cemetery to fill with pine needles and become a home for fungi.

The damp wind tore at Fletch's jacket. He shivered.

Or maybe it's something more sinister.

The gusts rattled the branches above his head until they sounded like bones.

Appropriate, mused Fletch. He pulled up his collar and continued studying the headstone inscriptions, looking for his several times great-great-grandfather.

According to the family stories, Captain Daring Dan O'Connell had been adventurous. He'd sailed from Liverpool to the Americas and beyond. Rumor had it his wealth had been acquired while working as a privateer—a genteel word for a pirate. But Fletch had little confidence in romanticized family tales. He suspected Daniel O'Connell had been an ordinary merchant.

He walked to the furthermost corner of the cemetery. After kneeling before a headstone worn almost unreadable by the elements, Fletch removed fallen tree branches and strips of bark. Grave now clear of debris, he spotted a row of pale, water-smoothed stones at the marker's foot. The center stone appeared to have eyes, a nose, and a grimacing mouth. The hair on his arms rose.

Fletch ran his fingertips across the headstone's lettering. Though it was a struggle, he was able to make out the epitaph: *Here lies Privateer Daring Dan O'Connell, husband, father, friend. He stole from some, killed one, and turned to good in the end.* Unfortunately, the birth and death dates were impossible to decipher.

Fletch stood. "So, you *were* a pirate," he mumbled.

He tried to memorize the gravestone poem to share with his parents, aunt, uncle, and countless cousins. Then he turned and hiked toward the cemetery's entrance.

A noise like a flag flapping in the wind caused him to pause and glance back at the cemetery's farthest corner.

A being with blacker-than-obsidian eyes stood beside Daring Dan's grave.

"Repenting late isn't always enough," it said, before picking up the stones in front of Daniel O'Connell's grave marker.

Suddenly, an unearthly howl filled the cemetery. Fletch wasn't sure if the howl came from the stone with the unhappy face, the dark-eyed creature, or the rising wind. But he *was* certain the laughter that followed came from the creature.

Once the coal-eyed being stopped laughing, it nodded, spread its leathery wings, leaped into the air, and vanished quick as lightning.

On shaky legs, Fletch raced back to his great-aunt and great-uncle's house. He didn't look back again.

Mummy

"...the corpse opened its eyes and winked very rapidly..."
– Some Words with a Mummy

Beneath the strips of faded linen
wrapped around my reclining form,
my bones grow restless.

Below my chest's dry, discolored flesh,
long ago coated with beeswax,
my heart beats slowly.

Beside my rib cage, bound so tightly
that lungs can barely expand,
my arms begin to stir.

Underneath head bandages treated
with pistachio resin,
my eyes flutter open.

Soon, I'll sit up. Then, stand and shuffle
into the dark, lonely night
searching for a warm meal.

Nonnie Winslow Crist
©2024

Strawman

"...there had been strange things narrated – fables I had always deemed them..."
– The Pit and the Pendulum

Diana studied her yard's Halloween decorations. There were filmy ghosts dangling from the limbs of a maple tree. Lining the edge of the driveway and sidewalk right up to the front door were strings of skull lights. Securely attached to the siding was a store-bought decoration that looked like a witch, carelessly riding her broom, had crashed into the house. Three black cats with their backs arched had been painted on wood and anchored in the grass with wooden stakes. And an autumn harvest display was spotlighted in the middle of the lawn.

What else do we need? she thought.

A scarecrow! The idea popped into her head like a piece of popcorn heated by a campfire. *But I need straw to build one.*

Deciding to use what resources she had, Diana stole straw from the harvest display. She thought no one would miss a few handfuls of straw taken from each of the bales stacked on the lawn between chrysanthemums, pumpkins, gourds, and bundled cornstalks.

Once she had a pile of straw ready, she went into the garage. Her father kept a container of old clothes in there to use for rags. When Dad worked on their car or lawn mower, he would usually get grease on his hands and need to wipe it off with a rag or two. So, storing rags in the garage made sense.

She rummaged through the rag bin and found a shirt, pair of pants, and mismatched socks. Then she looked through the garden supplies until she found a worn pair of her mother's flowered gloves and a hat.

Smiling like a jack-o-lantern, Diana put together her strawman.

Once the scarecrow was completed, she sat him on the middle bale of straw. To prevent him from tipping over, Diana moved two large pumpkins. By sitting one on either side of the strawman, she was able to keep him upright.

Diana stepped back and studied the harvest display with her scarecrow seated in the center.

"It looks great," she said. "But the scarecrow needs a head, and I don't have a lot of time left before Mom, Dad, and Grams arrive."

Her parents had gone across town to pick up Grams. Her grandmother didn't like to be alone on Halloween. All the kids running around in costumes and banging on her door made her nervous. Her parents and Grams would be home any minute. Not to mention, trick-or-treaters would be here soon.

With no time to actually make a scarecrow head from a pillowcase, Diana decided to improvise. She remembered her old, stuffed teddy bear was stored in the attic. Her father's brother, Uncle Jack, had won the oversized teddy at the local Volunteer Firemen's Carnival a few years ago. Diana had kept it in her room until she started middle school. Then, afraid her friends might think she was a baby, Diana had put the bear in the attic.

I don't need that stuffed animal anymore, she decided. *I'll cut the bear's head off and use it for the strawman.*

Scissors in hand, Diana climbed the stairs to the attic. The attic door creaked as she pushed it open. After flicking on the light, she quickly found the teddy bear. With only a moment of sadness for the end of a once loved stuffed animal, she poked the scissors into the bear's neck. She was surprised to discover it wasn't difficult to snip open the seam holding the head onto the furry body.

"Sorry, Teddy," Diana called to the bear's body as, carrying its fuzzy head, she turned off the light, closed the attic door, and clamored down the stairs.

Quick as a wink, she went outside, crossed the lawn, and placed the bear's head between the scarecrow's shoulders about where a neck should be. Then, she placed Mom's rattiest looking garden hat on top of the stuffed bear head.

"You look amazing, Mr. Strawman!" she exclaimed as her parents' car pulled into the driveway.

"Ooo! That's one scary scarecrow," said Dad as he climbed out of the car.

"You mean scare-*bear* don't you?" said Mom.

Then Diana and her parents laughed.

Grams did not laugh. She wagged her finger at Diana. "I don't know where you got that head from, but it looks demented. In my day, if someone put something like that on their front lawn, we would have..."

Whatever Grams meant to say next was left unsaid.

"Oh, Grams. It's just some Halloween fun," said Mom. "Come on, let's go inside and have dinner before the trick-or-treaters get here."

***

More than a hundred kids dressed in costumes and masks knocked on Diana's door. She handed out candy and told the youngest children they looked good. Many of the older kids made comments about her scare-bear. Her favorite comment was made by Wilson, a fourth grader who lived two doors down.

Wilson had said, "That bear-headed scarecrow is going to give kids nightmares." Then, he had shivered and added, "Even big kids like me."

Diana had giggled. "Don't be silly," she'd told Wilson. But even as she said it, she supposed her scare-bear was a little creepy. But creepy was what October thirty-first was all about. Who cares if she had to decapitate a stuffed animal to build her strawman?

By nine o'clock, trick-or-treating was done. Diana went upstairs to her bedroom to read and then go to sleep. Unfortunately, Halloween had fallen on a Wednesday. She'd have to get up early and go to school tomorrow.

***

The next morning, Diana didn't come down for breakfast. Her mother went to her bedroom. She gasped when she saw a bear-faced strawman sitting on the floor beside Diana's bed. And when she pulled back the covers, she screamed.

For there, with her eyes wide open, laid Diana with a fuzzy paw over her nose and mouth. She had been smothered by her old, now headless, stuffed Teddy.

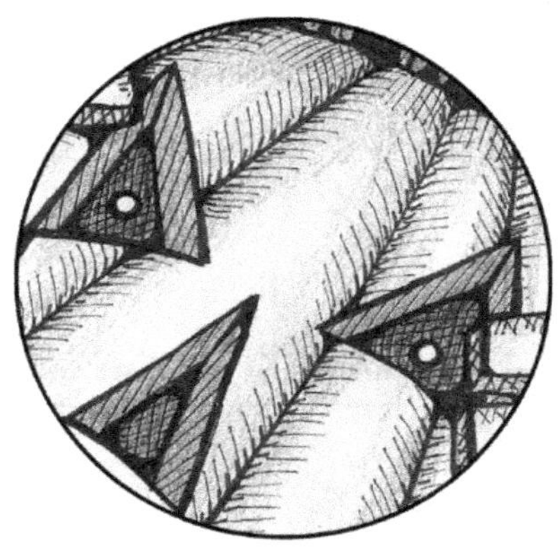

© 2024
Vonnie Winslow Crist

Candy Cottage

"...amid the rich October leaves of the forest..."
– Morella

Ben pointed at a distant house. It was at the end of the cul-de-sac, down a dirt lane, and only visible in the darkness because of a bonfire roaring on the front lawn. The house appeared to be decorated with huge pieces of candy and slabs of gingerbread.

"Cool decorations," he told his friend, Robert. "I bet they're giving away the good stuff."

"Yeah!" said Robert. "I know it's after eight o'clock, but we'll make this the last house we visit."

"Our parents won't mind if we're a few minutes late," said Ben. "Race you," he added before taking off at a run.

Bags in hand, Ben and Robert ran down the driveway to the gingerbread and candy covered cottage. They knocked on its door.

"Trick-or-treat," they shouted when the door opened.

"Welcome, welcome," said a lady dressed in black. "Come inside, boys. Grab some sweets."

Though they'd been told not to enter anyone's home, they spotted the kitchen table stacked high with chocolate bars. Eager for handfuls of the good stuff, they went in.

Suddenly, the woman grabbed the boys by their hair. Cackling loudly, she tossed them into a large, steel cage and slammed the door shut.*

Before Ben and Robert could react, she turned a key in the door's lock. Then she dropped the key into her sweater's pocket.

"You may have all the candy bars you want," she promised them as she tossed one chocolate bar after another into the cage. "Then, when you're fat enough, I shall roast you for my dinner."

"Please, let us go," cried the boys.

"No, dearies," said the woman. "It gets harder every year to lure trick-or-treaters down my lane. But now that I have you two, I shall put out the bonfire." She laughed and added, "You see, unlike you two, I am *not* greedy."

Terrified, Ben and Robert realized their mistake. Hoping to stay thin for a long time, they lost their appetite for Halloween candy—no matter how tasty.

*You can lean forward and clap your hands loudly one time.

Fairy

"...scarcely discernible in the brilliant atmosphere...floated a pair of the most delicately imagined wings..."
– The Assignation

Ignoring their parents' instructions, Mo and David cut through the church parking lot and graveyard. Taking the shortcut lessened the time it took to get to the soccer field by more than five minutes.

"Nobody will know," David assured his sister. "We can use the sidewalk on the way home if you'd like."

Mo shook her head. "I hate lying to Mom and Dad."

"We don't need to lie," said David, "unless they ask."

Mo sighed but didn't argue.

As they passed through the graveyard, David spotted a woman dressed in pink ballet slippers, tights, and a puffy dress prying open a casket with a shovel. He froze.

"What's wrong?" asked his sister.

He pointed at the woman.

"She's a fairy," whispered Mo. "Look at her wings."

Before he could reply, the fairy looked up. She seemed surprised to see anyone on a Tuesday afternoon. After tucking a strand of golden hair behind her ear, she batted her eyelashes and smiled.

"What are you two doing here?" she inquired in a voice so sweet it reminded David of a bird singing.

"We're going to meet some friends," he replied.

"I don't usually rob the dead," explained the fairy as she pointed to the casket and fluttered her gossamer wings. "But my castle has developed structural problems."

"Your castle?" David scowled. He had no experience with fairies. Therefore, he didn't know whether this one was telling the truth or trying to pull the wool over his eyes.

"Yes," replied the fairy. "It's a fabulous structure built of the teeth I find under the pillows of children. It has soaring towers, arched windows, and a great hall. Alas, the foundation of the west tower is crumbling. So, I need thousands of teeth to repair it."

"Let's get out of here," whispered Mo as she turned, then sprinted in the direction of the field where their friends waited.

"Of course, if you'd like to donate a few teeth," said the fairy, "I'm happy to pull them." She took a pair of glittering pliers from a pink, sequined knapsack resting beside the casket.

"No!" shouted David.

Heart beating faster than a dentist's drill, he raced after his sister. He knew if he tripped, the fairy and her pliers would grab a few of his teeth. So worried was he that David didn't see the tree root until *after* his toe caught under it.

Yvonnie Winslow-Crist
©2024

Holly

"...a ghost, amid the entombing trees..."
– To Helen

"It's too cold to search the woods for greens," said Nathaniel. He pulled his knit hat down over his ears, then picked up a large plastic bag.

"Mom said to bring back pine, spruce, and holly for decorating," Gabriel reminded his brother. "I don't think she cares that it's cold."

"It's nearly dusk. We could save time," suggested Nathaniel, "by going across the street to the churchyard."

"I don't think that's a good idea." Gabriel shook his head. "I know there are lots of evergreen trees there, but we might get in trouble."

"We could ask the minister," said Nathaniel as he crossed the street and walked up to the parsonage's door.

Gabriel followed.

Nathaniel knocked on the door. A few seconds later, it swung open.

"Hello, boys," said the minister's wife, Mrs. Shuttleworthy. "Can I help you?"

"Hello, Mrs. Shuttleworthy," said Nathaniel. "Gabriel and I were wondering if it would be okay for us to cut a few greens from the churchyard for Christmas decorations?"

"I don't see why not." The minister's wife smiled. "Those shrubs and trees need to be trimmed anyway. But you'd better hurry. It's getting dark."

"Thanks," replied Nathaniel before he turned and jogged toward the church.

Gabriel ran behind his brother. "I'm still not sure this is a good idea," he muttered.

"You worry too much," said Nathaniel as he pulled a pair of garden shears from one of his puffy jacket's pockets.

Gabriel shrugged his shoulders, then took a pair of garden shears from his coat pocket. He joined his brother in snipping sprigs of pine, spruce, boxwood, hemlock, fir, and other greens from the churchyard's trees and bushes. Nathaniel was probably right. He *did* worry too much.

When both of their bags were nearly full, Nathaniel pointed with his shears at the church's graveyard.

"There's some holly," he said as he opened the graveyard's gate. "It's the last kind of greenery Mom asked for."

"We can't take holly from someone's grave." Gabriel shivered. "It's like stealing from the dead."

"Don't be silly," replied Nathaniel as he cut sprigs from a large holly bush. "What use do the dead have for holly branches?"

"I don't know," answered Gabriel in a quiet voice as he noticed the holly's gnarled roots grew into several graves. With every snip of his shears, he felt his heart beating faster.

"Done," stated Nathaniel.

He looked at his brother and opened his mouth to speak. But no sound came out. Raising his garden shears, he pointed at a spot beside the holly bush.

"What's wrong with you?" Nathaniel frowned.

"The dead *do* care if we steal their holly," he finally managed to say.

Nathaniel glanced at the spot where Gabriel was pointing. Hovering above the ground was a pale woman in an old-fashioned dress. In her hand she held a withered holly sprig.

"Ah!" screamed Nathaniel.

"Ah!" yelled Gabriel.

They grabbed their bags of greens and raced home.

Later that night, after their mother had decorated the house with branchlets of pine, fir, spruce, boxwood, hemlock, and holly, the boys sat quietly on the sofa. Neither spoke as they stared at the ghostly woman floating in the corner of the room.

She smiled a toothless smile at them. Then, she waved a sprig of dead holly.

"Do you think she'll go back to the graveyard?" whispered Gabriel.

Nathaniel shook his head. "We brought more than greenery home. I think she's here to stay."

"Here to stay," promised the ghost as she dropped the holly and rushed toward the brothers with arms outstretched.

Field Trip

"...he seated himself at a small table, on which were a pen and ink..."
– The Gold Bug

This year's fifth grade field trip was to Baltimore. Many students were excited to see Ravens' Stadium. Some students, like Aria and her friend, Kenna, were just as excited to visit the grave of the writer Edgar Allan Poe, the catacombs under Westminster Hall, and the house on Amity Street where Poe had lived.

When they climbed out of the bus, their teachers, Mrs. Thompson and Ms. Smyth, divided the fifth-grade class into six groups of four.

"Stay in your groups, especially when we go into the house where Edgar Allan Poe lived with his wife, Virginia, and his mother-in-law, Mrs. Clemm," Mrs. Thompson told the class.

"The house is small," explained Ms. Smyth. "Only one group at a time will be allowed to go upstairs to the room where Poe wrote some of his stories and poems."

"How long do we *have* to stay here?" asked Robert Holland.

Aria rolled her eyes. Robert was always impatient.

"Just long enough for everyone to visit the attic and look around the rest of the house," replied Ms. Smyth. "Then, it's off to the gravesite."

"Yeah!" hollered a couple of boys.

"Stay on the sidewalk until we get inside," ordered Mrs. Thompson as the noisy boys started pushing one another.

Moments later, the class was inside the Poe house's living and dining rooms.

"This is amazing," said Aria.

"And a little spooky," added Kenna.

Aria shook her head. Though Kenna was kind and funny, she wasn't very brave.

"Just wait until we get to the burial grounds and catacombs," said Aria. "*Then*, you might have something to be scared about."

Kenna wrapped her arms around herself and pretended to shiver.

Both girls laughed.

Finally, it was their turn to climb up the narrow stairway and visit the attic. The other two girls in their group hurried up the steps, looked quickly into the attic room, then clumped down the steps. Aria and Kenna took their time. They studied the little room with its tiny window.

"It's small and lonely," said Kenna with a sigh before heading back down to the dining room.

Aria lingered. She liked to read frightening stories. She knew the Baltimore Ravens football team got their name from one of Edgar Allan Poe's poems. She'd heard Poe died young and didn't even have a grave marker for years.

No wonder he always looks so sad in pictures, she thought.

Studying a quill pen and ink bottle sitting on the wooden writing desk one last time before joining her classmates, Aria witnessed the figure of a man appear out of thin air. He was dressed in outdated clothes and had dark hair. Aria realized she could see through him.

About to call for Kenna or Ms. Smyth or Mrs. Thompson, Aria fell silent when the man turned, raised his hand, and whispered, "Hush."*

Then, with grief-filled eyes, he stared at her and murmured, "My soul shall be lifted, nevermore."

"I'm sorry, Mr. Poe," Aria replied as she backed down the stairs.

The ghost nodded, then disappeared.

All of a sudden, Aria wasn't as thrilled to visit Poe's grave and the catacombs as she'd been earlier in the day.

Because, she thought, *I don't know who or what I might see there!*

*If you are reading this to someone, you can raise your hand and reach toward them when you say this.

From the Author

Since a young age, I have listened to, read, and imagined scary tales. All the stories, poems, and illustrations in *Shivers, Scares, and Chills* came from my imagination. Some of them began with folklore, superstitions, and urban legends. All of them have a pinch of inspiration from the life and work of American writer, Edgar Allan Poe. After each title is a Poe quote that helped inspire it.

You can check the Notes section to read more about the beginning places for the stories and poems. I challenge older readers to figure out the extra Edgar Allan Poe Connection (EPC) in each tale.

I hope you enjoy my spooky words and drawings.

– Vonnie Winslow Crist

Notes and
Edgar Allan Poe Connections

1. Rabbits: A person must wear special glasses when looking at a solar eclipse to prevent eye damage. I wondered what happened to animals who looked at the sun during an eclipse without those glasses.
Edgar Allan Poe Connection (EPC): Barry is a name from Poe's short story, "Loss of Breath."
2. Flittermice: The sound of the wind in a chimney can be strange. The sound of bats leaving at dusk can be scary. But what if it's something else making the noise?
EPC: Cammie (a nickname for Camille) and Pauline are people in Poe's short story, "The Murders in the Rue Morgue." The name Lee-Lee is from Poe's poem, "Annabel Lee."
3. Redcap: Redcap is a goblin from folklore who dyes his cap red using the blood of his victims.
EPC: Harry is a name from Poe's satirical short story, "Some Words with a Mummy."
4. Toads: Mushrooms or toadstools sometimes grow in circles. According to folklore, these "fairy rings" are magical places where fairies, elves, pixies, witches, and even toads dance by the light of the full moon.
EPC: The names Tabitha and Kathleen appear in Poe's satirical story, "The Man That Was Used Up."

5. Marbles: One of my grandfathers died when I was young. I liked to think he was watching over me. And I still have my green glass shooter marble.
EPC: The name William is from Poe's short story, "William Wilson." Both the names Talbot and Simpson come from another of Poe's short stories, "The Spectacles."
6. Feeding the Fish: Growing up, my dad would drive my sisters and me to Loch Raven Reservoir. We'd bring a bag of stale bread and toss pieces to the fish swimming by the platform near the dam.
EPC: The brother and sister are named for Edgar Allan Poe (Eddie) and the title character of his poem, "Annabel Lee."
7. Dowsing: Dowsers or water witches use a forked branch or two metal wires to find water below ground.
EPC: The name Roderick comes from Poe's short story, "The Fall of the House of Usher," and Legrand is from his story, "The Gold Bug." Fraser and Jonesy (a nickname for Jones) are names in Poe's story, "Lionizing."
8. Mossy Bog: There are many legends of mysterious creatures or cryptids in bogs, swamps, marshes, and bayous.
EPC: The names Verds, Augustus, Gordon, and Polly are from Poe's only novel, *The Narrative of Arthur Gordon Pym of Nantucket*.
9. Ravens: Ravens are scavengers. An unkindness of ravens will gobble up roadkill, graveyard worms and beetles, or an unburied body.
EPC: "The Raven" is probably Poe's most well-known poem.
10. Pop's Teeth: My grandfather soaked his dentures in a jar beside his bed. I was never brave enough to touch them!
EPC: Teeth play an important role in Poe's short story, "Berenice." Bella's name is short for Arabella, a character in Poe's satirical story, "The Man That Was Used Up." Nico (short for Nicolino) and Curtis are names from Poe's story, "The Oblong Box."
11. Mid-Eclipse: The moon can turn a reddish color during a lunar eclipse. According to folklore, werewolves are humans who turn to wolves when the moon is full.

EPC: John is a character in Poe's satirical story, "The Man That Was Used Up," and Gruff was a character in his story, "The Business Man."

12. It Tickles: It's a superstition that if your ear itches, someone is talking about you. A spider nesting in a person's face is an urban legend.

EPC: The name Lily comes from its mention in Poe's poem, "Dream-Land." The uncle's name, Bransby, comes from Poe's short story, "William Wilson."

13. Northern Lights: The aurora borealis or northern lights happen when solar winds enter earth's upper atmosphere. Little, large-eyed, gray-skinned aliens who abduct people are an urban legend.

EPC: Hans is a name from Poe's story, "Hans Phaall." Bobby Tompkins is a name from his story, "The Business Man."

14. Swimming Alone: A longstanding rule is to never swim alone. A kelpie, also known as a water-horse, is a mythical creature which lures swimmers to their death.

EPC: The friends' names come from Poe's poems "To Helen," "For Annie," and "Elizabeth." The name of the main character, Mary, is from his story, "Metzengerstein." The name of the lake comes from Poe's story, "How to Write a Blackwood Article."

15. Black Dog: Folklore says it's bad luck for a black cat to cross your path. But as the saying goes: "See a penny pick it up. All day long you'll have good luck." Black dogs appear in the folklore of many cultures. Sometimes, they are evil. Other times, black dogs are tricksters or can even help lost travelers.

EPC: Thomas is a name from Poe's short story, "The Assignation" and his satirical story, "The Man That Was Used Up." Lyttleton is a name from Poe's story, "Loss of Breath."

16. Bells: Years ago, strings which led to bells *were* attached to the wrists of bodies. Nowadays, doctors are much better at determining if a person is dead.

EPC: A fear of Edgar Allan Poe's was being buried alive as we learn from several of his stories, including "The

Premature Burial." Tom Dobson is a name from Poe's short story, "The Business Man." The name Violet comes from his poem, "The Valley of Unrest," and Ginny, a nickname for Virginia, comes from Poe's poem, "Sonnet – To My Mother."

17. Gargoyles in the Garden: I've always imagined the concrete gargoyle statues in my garden coming to life. A skogtroll is a forest troll. Baba Yaga is an Eastern European magical, witch-like character. In a Mother Goose nursery rhyme, an old woman is tossed into the sky so she can sweep away the cobwebs.

EPC: Charley (a nickname for Charles) and Pennifeather are names from Poe's short story, "Thou Art The Man."

18. Giggles: Coulrophobia is the fear of clowns. While I am not a fan of clowns, I don't *think* I'm a coulrophobic.

EPC: The names Joel and Mr. Pym are from Poe's only novel, *The Narrative of Arthur Gordon Pym of Nantucket.*

19. Watching: Often, I get a feeling that something or someone is watching me.

EPC: Sometimes, Poe has the narrator or main character in his stories watch the action unfold. An example would be the narrator (and eventual murderer) in his short story, "The Tell-Tale Heart."

20. Crickets: Folklore says it's lucky to have a cricket on your hearth. Superstition promises if you kill a cricket, you'll have seven years of bad luck.

EPC: Miranda, nicknamed Randi, is a name from Poe's story, "The Man That Was Used Up."

21. Looking for Daniel O'Connell: I like to investigate family stories to see if they're fact or fiction.

EPC: The name Fletcher is from Poe's poem, "The Landscape Garden" and Daniel O'Connell comes from his humorous story, "Diddling."

22. Mummy: I put myself in the place of a mummy that's come to life.

EPC: In Poe's story, "Some Words With A Mummy," the mummy is alive beneath its bandages and begins to talk.

23. Strawman: This Halloween story, where people are in costumes, celebration is in the air, and someone is

smothered for wronging the murderer, was inspired by Poe's revenge tale, "The Cask of Amontillado."

EPC: Diana is a name from Poe's humorous story, "A Predicament," and Wilson is a name from his story, "William Wilson."

24. Candy Cottage: This story is a twist on trick-or-treating and the Hansel and Gretel tale.

EPC: Ben (short for Bentley) and Robert are two names from Poe's short story, "Lionizing."

25. Fairy: The Tooth Fairy is a folklore and fairy tale being who collects baby teeth from children after they fall out. But what if she needed lots of teeth quickly?

EPC: Mo (short for Morella) is a name from Poe's story, "Morella." David is a name from his story, "A Tale of Jerusalem."

26. Holly: An evergreen, holly represents eternal life and the hope of rebirth. In urban legends and folklore, there is always a penalty for stealing from the dead.

EPC: Ghosts and ghostly figures appear often in Edgar Allan Poe's writing. Shuttleworthy is a name from Poe's short story, "Thou Art the Man."

24. Field Trip: I have visited Edgar Allan Poe's tiny home on Amity Street in Baltimore. Even a small group of students would need to be broken into groups for a tour.

EPC: The teachers' names Thompson and Smyth (an alternate spelling of Smith) are names from Poe's short story, "The Man That Was Used Up." Robert Holland is a name from Poe's fictitious story presented as an article, "The Balloon Hoax." And the words Poe's ghost says in the story are from his poem, "The Raven."

Acknowledgements

Thanks to Dawn Schiavone Crist for her friendship and invaluable critiquing, Andrea Thomas for insightful editing, and Dark Owl Publishing for taking a chance on a book of shivery, scary, bone-chilling stories. Thank you to my friends and family for supporting my creative endeavors and patiently listening to me spin fantastical tales. Lastly, a special thanks to Ernie for always being there.

About the Author

Born in the Year of the Dragon, Vonnie Winslow Crist, MS Professional Writing, has had a lifelong interest in reading, writing, art, science fiction, myth, fairy tales, folklore, and legends. An award-winning author and illustrator, she is a member of the Science Fiction & Fantasy Writers Association, Horror Writers Association, Society of Children's Book Writers & Illustrators, and National League of American Pen Women. Her first book in the Shivers and Scares series, *Shivers, Scares, and Goosebumps*, won the 2023 Best Children's Book Imaginarium Imadjinn Award. Her speculative stories and poems have been published in Italy, Spain, Finland, Germany, India, Australia, Japan, Canada, the UK, and the USA.

A cloverhand who believes the world is still filled with mystery, magic, and miracles, she loves to hear from readers at conventions, conferences, and online. Visit her website at www.vonniewinslowcrist.com or connect with her on Facebook: www.facebook.com/WriterVonnieWinslowCrist.

www.ingramcontent.com/pod-product-compliance
Lightning Source LLC
LaVergne TN
LVHW010102110826
845155LV00028B/455

* 9 7 8 1 9 5 1 7 1 6 4 2 4 *